Henry and the Great Society

Henry and the Great Society

A NOVEL

H. L. ROUSH, SR.

HENRY AND THE GREAT SOCIETY

Printed in the United States of America.

Library of Congress Cataloging in Publication Data

Roush, Herbert L., 1925-
Henry and the Great Society.

1. Title.
PZ4.R858He 1977 [PS3568.0888] 813'.5'4 77-12822
ISBN 0-89293-048-9

For Information about other books and cd's, contact:

JESUS Loves Me Ministry

3587 Clover Lane
New Castle, PA 16105
(412) 658-5180
FAX (724) 658-2940
Web Site: http://www.jesuslovesme.org
Email: info@jesuslovesme.org

Henry and the Great Society

DEDICATION

There is, among men, a universal longing to go back to the earth from whence they came. Man will never forget his native place in Paradise lost, nor will he ever cease to yearn for a life of perfect contentment. The hope that occupies every heart is the secret dream of a Shangri-La discovered where there is an escape from the pressures of this present society. Each of us, in this insane world in which we live, knows something of the restlessness and the dissatisfaction that create a relentless obsession to escape the treadmill of existence this society has forced upon us—an existence that has crushed us with pressures and demands that far exceed our resources; a life that often shatters our peace and leaves us like trapped animals, pacing the cage of our circumstances, plotting how to break the iron bands of involvement. We have all known the frustrations of our self-imposed timetables and commitments that cause us to feel like wheat in the grist mill of an evil system; a system that crushes our hopes, dreams, desires and blows away, like chaff, the highest aspirations of our souls.

As has been said before: "I write with no higher hopes than motivate the rooster at daybreak—I do not expect to be appreciated or even tolerated, but I hope to awaken some to a new day." And so, to those who are homesick and do not realize that the "home" for which they are longing is not a geographical location, but a way of life, I sincerely dedicate this small effort. Especially do I dedicate this book to those whose homesickness will never be cured on this earth. May we all know the truth and by the knowledge of that truth be set FREE.

INTRODUCTION

As I sit at my typewriter about to begin this book, I am searching for some justification for its existence. One of history's wisest men once wrote at the conclusion of his book, ". . . of making of books there is no end; and much study is a weariness of the flesh" (Ecclesiastes 12:12b). These words convince me of his unquestionable wisdom. I have no idea how many millions of books there are now on record in the libraries of the world nor how many thousands more are being prepared for publication at this time. Every subject that ever entered the mind of man has been recorded by someone for future minds to pursue. Most books cover the same themes and say the same things that have been said a thousand times before by much wiser men, yet men continue to flood the earth with millions of books. Mine will be no different from theirs.

It has been well said that paper will lie still and one can write anything on it. I am wondering why I should impose upon this perfectly good paper the words I am about to write. There are two reasons, I have decided. First, that is what paper is for, to write words on; and the purpose of writing words is that others might read them. Second, and far more important, when a man has a fire burning in his bones, he has to put it out. When he is possessed of a woe upon his heart, he can do nothing but preach it. When he is filled up inside to the bursting point, he must purge his system of it all or it will crush him. He cares not whether it is read or heeded, but he must hear himself say the things he has been made to believe. This is why my dog arouses at night to bark at a passing train. He does not hope that it will stop, or even slow as it crosses the path of his life at a distance; nor does he imagine that all on that train have heard his voice and are meditating on his message; he only does what he knows he *must* do. I am about to do what I know I must do with the story of "Henry and the Great Society"—tell it to you, my readers. It will be for you to decide if I have told in any way a part of your own story or if Henry is really the story of my own poor life. Whatever the case, I beg your indulgence in my desire to bark at the train of your life; and afterward, you may go back to your sleep, if you can.

TABLE OF CONTENTS

Chapter I

HENRY'S WORLD

Somehow when the county commissioners improved the main roads of Mindoah County, they must have forgotten about the old Salem Pike; for it still looked much like it did when Union troops rode by on their way to meet General Early in the Shenondoah. Oh, it had changed some, as all things do. It wasn't as wide, for the spreading brush and shrubbery on the right-of-way had nibbled away at the road for the past 100 years. The ruts didn't get as deep as they did then, for many wagonloads of stone from nearby Sycamore Creek had made their presence felt over the years. And then, there wasn't as much traffic as in the old days. I always supposed that this was why the good commissioners, in their freshly starched wash pants and wide police suspenders, decided to abandon old Salem Pike. After all, in all the ten miles of its meandering through hollows, seeking the course of least resistance, there were only seven farms; and at the sudden end there was Willoughby.

Willoughby was at best only a settlement and it lay at the end of the freshly gravelled road that came from the county seat 30 miles away. The little community boasted only ten houses in all clustered around its single business, a large weathered general store. There wasn't much excitement in Willoughby, but there was at least a daily routine. Four passenger trains a day came through and one even slowed enough to catch the single mail pouch a day that left the town and to throw off in its place the incoming mail as the train thundered east. The day was more or less regulated by those four trains, known affectionately as "Old 31," "Number 12," "Decatur Express," and the town favorite, "The Cannonball," because of the determined way it hurtled through Willoughby ignoring even the town dogs who ran alongside barking at its intrusion. Religiously the folks gathered daily at P. T. Wigal's General Store to do their trading and then hang around to drift to the door of the porch to watch "Number 12" come through, and to wave vigorously at the engineer whose name no one ever knew.

Every day was pretty much the same in Willoughby, but there was time . . . Time for Mr. Wigal to plant and tend a luxurious garden next to his store and time in the midst of a sale to ". . . step outside and take a look at my beans and 'taters'. . . ." There was also time after waiting on Widow Abbot to inquire about her health and time to listen to her detailed description of her latest bout with arthritis and time to think about it later and to wonder if there was anything he could do to make her life a little more bearable. There was time to sit around the old cherry-red Burnside stove on a winter evening at Wigal's to trade knives and pocket watches and small talk about the day's events.

It was just like old Mr. Wigal said many times, "What's your hurry? There ain't no place to go." He was right. He hadn't found any place to go for 60 years, mainly because he wasn't looking for any place to go. His father had gone in the store business back in '91 in that same building, and Mr. Wigal was born and reared in Willoughby, and never supposed that he would do anything else than take over the store when his father died. Oh, he'd like to retire someday, but he never could figure out what to do about the store business. Nobody else wanted to take it over, and what would Willoughby be without P. T. Wigal's General Store?—with its straight-board benches on the porch, hand carved by a thousand pocket knives in the hands of old friends; some now lay silent in the little town cemetery behind the M. E. Church on the hill overlooking Willoughby. And if there was no store, where would the town meetings be held, instead of around the old Burnside in winter? So life was free, and time was plentiful; and most everyone who lived there liked it.

The big American flag that hung wound by the wind around its staff atop the general store was the only silent reminder of the presence of the Federal Government in all the area and marked the location of the post office. I guess you would call it an "office"—it was actually only a screened corner of the feed room, and the bags of sweet smelling horse and mule feed, chicken mash, and Red Dog gave a distinctive odor of their own. Clayton Peters had carried the mail out of this "office" on the Salem Pike for 27. years and owned the only good saddle horse in the community. He never let anyone forget it either; always challenging everyone in general, and no one in particular, to a horse race, knowing all the while that the only horses around were work horses. Clayton was a welcome sight as he rode the pike each day on his big bay horse, who knew every one of the stops better than Clayton did, which allowed him to take a little nap between stops. This was only necessary if the domino game lasted longer than usual the night before at Wigal's; or if his big bay, named Ted, had ridden the fence down and Clayton was forced out of bed in the middle of the night to fetch him from Howard's corn patch next door. Clayton often brought to someone on the route a bag of flour, a box of salt, or some other small item needed before Saturday, and they always remembered Ted with a bite of sugar or apple; and sometimes, if the weather was nasty, they would even ask Clayton in for a cup of coffee.

Most of the patrons on the route were old folks whose children had grown and moved away. The farms themselves told the story: a piece of loose tin flapping on the barn roof, a weathered fence around the yard, the grass grown high in the summer and the ball field in the pasture below the barn grown over in weeds. Most of the young folks had migrated the 30 miles or more to the county seat, Chamberstown, where the pottery had once been the main industry. I say once, for Chamberstown was growing for the first time in its 130 years of existence. General Electronics had recently chosen it for the site of a new plant said to cost 150 million dollars which was more money than was on the tax books in Mindoah County. With the new industry had come its related blessings, through tax revenue, of new and improved highways, schools and a reformed city government. The large plywood sign at the corporation limits proudly displayed these facts and informed motorists passing through that this was the fastest growing city in the Seminole Valley. The Chamber of Commerce and the Kiwanis, Rotary and Lion's clubs were happily organizing the civic-minded folk and performing face-lifting miracles that would attract more industry and bring with them more jobs, money and progress—a thing they said was badly needed in the Valley. Chamberstown would soon boast its own swimming pool, golf course, city park and Big Burger Drive-In. The old stone courthouse at the foot of Main Street looked on all the flurry of this thing called progress with a somber countenance; but its four-faced tower clock faithfully tolled the hour with a gruff voice, as it had done for the Union Army on its way to the Shenandoah. But this was another world and was miles away from Willoughby, Salem Pike and Henry Morgan.

Chapter II

HENRY'S HOME

I said that most of the patrons along the dirt pike from Willoughby were old folks, and they were, but Henry wasn't. He looked younger than his 40 years and his wife Esther had the blush of youth upon her round face. Their three children, Brent, Jeff and Hilda, were barefoot and suntanned in the summertime, rosy-cheeked in the wintertime and shy, polite and happy all the time. They had reason to be. Henry was a thoughtful, quiet man who had never felt the panic that had driven his friends to abandon the farm for the glories of Chamberstown and its progress. It wasn't that Henry was opposed to progress as much as it was that he sincerely questioned the value of its fruit. But, well, maybe it will be better understood if I tell it to you like Henry told it to me.

The way he felt about it was this: his father and his grandfather before him had lived well off the 160 acres which Henry now owned by inheritance, and he felt the land would be just as good for him. When he married Esther Jenkins from the adjoining farm, she felt as strongly about it as Henry did and both looked forward to raising their children on Salem Pike as they had been raised. They lived pretty much as their parents had and saw no reason to change much of anything. Oh, they whitewashed the tree trunks in the front yard and replaced the pickets in the yard fence (some of which Henry himself had broken as a growing boy chasing Old Tippy, who was chasing the old White Leghorn rooster through the fence). They painted the weather boarding of the large double-porch, two-story house, and its tin roof shone bright red in the morning sun as though it was shouting to the world that a new family lived here now. It seemed like just a few months ago, instead of years, that Henry and Esther had sat at the kitchen table doodling on a sheet of tablet paper trying to come up with a name for the place. They finally did, and the sign hung proudly on the large pine tree just inside the front gate with its hand-lettered message, "Whispering Pines."

They had deep roots there—as deep as the old pine Henry's grandfather had planted by the gate the day he brought his bride to Salem Pike and a new house. Life was complete there, and they seldom had call to go anywhere; when they did it was usually only as far as Willoughby.

The electric line had never come out the pike and, having never known its convenience, Henry had never felt its loss. The kerosene lamps seemed to be sufficient for all the evening activities and the Aladdin lamps stood by, like sentries awaiting the call to special duty, to light every corner of the large living room. Of course, the wicks of the regular lamps had to be trimmed occasionally, and once in a while the chimneys had to be washed and wiped dry with old newspaper. A few candles were kept handy in the buffet drawer for special occasions like Christmas, or birthdays, or to light the ugly face of a Jack-o-lantern carved with Henry's Barlow knife. The barn lanterns hung ready on the back porch for emergencies, such as as a cow about to be fresh, a skunk in the chicken house, a mare about to foal, or the excitement of some woods creature challenged at the edge of the yard by Old Brown, a descendent of Old Tippy. Nobody knew who Old Brown's daddy was, and nobody cared. Henry's gum boots, along with three small pairs, stood proudly at attention in their place by the screen door; and his denim jacket and sweat-stained straw hat hung on a wooden peg carved by his grandfather and worn smooth by 75 years of jackets and sweaty hats.

Lack of electricity was no real problem to Henry and Esther; especially in the summer when after a full day's work in the sun they welcomed the cool and the darkness of the evening. They never thought of lighting a lamp for the porch; for the light would only have drawn the mosquitos and millers to torment them, and the heat would have been an unwelcome visitor. They loved to sit on the porch in the summer evenings and feel the darkness fall around them like a welcome rain as it tucked all nature to bed.

Who can describe the sights and sounds of such an evening? . . . the shimmering quicksilver of a full moon, the spattering of stars across a black sky, the clouds slipping across the face of the moon like a bashful lady covering her face with a fan. In the distance, the plaintive cry of a lonesome whippoorwill, the endless chorus of the tree frogs (or toads such as the case may be and a common topic of conversation between Brent and Hilda). Occasionally, as though he were diligently watching the score of this nocturnal symphony, a giant bull frog would explode in a massive "Whomp!!" and somewhere from the banks of Sycamore Creek behind the house, from his hidden place in one of the many trees that lined its bank, a screech owl would render his weird solo. If he was especially haunting in his cry, Hilda would run to the lap of Esther and snuggle close complaining that she was chilly, although the boys said she was afraid, like all girls. Henry liked to say that the night was God's tranquilizer.

And there was talk, or as they say nowadays, communication. Winter was filled with it, for everything had slowed to a walk; and the evenings were long before the fireplace and rich in special talk . . . open and intimate discussions on the questions of life and death, right and wrong, moral and immoral. There were the frivolous interruptions of the children, when the talk was serious, that betrayed a searching mind and a longing heart. There was light fun-filled talk that invented new riddles, or composed new poems, or solved hard puzzles. Then there was that special time when Henry would give in to the pressure of the children to tell one of his now-famous stories. Sometimes they were the modified stories of his own life that always had a moral; but as often as not they were the product of a fertile imagination that could invent pirates and Indians, wild animals and heroes with equal ease. The children would sit spellbound and open-mouthed; and always, Henry became in those stories the bravest, strongest, smartest man in the world.

When bedtime came, there was often the gathering at the kitchen table for a cold cup of milk; and then around the lighted lamp, a few verses from the Book of Books, more questions and a bedtime prayer. After lingering kisses that reflected a pleasant evening ended too soon, the children followed Esther with her lamp up the open stairs to their beds to settle deep in the straw and feather ticks. Henry and Esther would retire to the porch, if in summer, for a last few moments together . . . sort of a time when they said the things that need to be said over and over again, and thought about the things that need to be thought about often; and there was a closeness between them that was good and right. There wasn't always talk at that time. Sometimes there was just a contented silence, and Henry used to say, "Listen to it. It has a soothing sound of its own," and it was broken only by the sounds of nature's night noises quieting their hearts and minds. The only sound of man that could be heard was the regular squeak of the swing chain grating on its rusty and worn hook and the steady rhythm of Esther's hickory rocker.

Chapter III

HENRY'S LIFE

Morning at Whispering Pines usually began with the arrogant voice of "Big Red" the rooster, named by Jeff and respected since he last flogged Brent for entering his domain unannounced. Big Red would croak out his message with no concern as to whether he was heard or not, and his hens would answer with contented clucking; and they were answered by the busy peeps of the chicks. In the distance, the early morning caws of crows flying patrol over the edge of the woods nearby could be heard, and, if in the spring, the shrill excited nicker of a colt only 30 feet away from its disinterested mother, but sure it was lost forever. The patient and never-discouraged bobwhite and the soft cooing of the mourning doves would call all to a brand new day, and this faithful alarm clock never had to be wound or set. Often, as Henry would lie there in the early morning, thinking over the day's work ahead, he would hear the steady and subdued sound of Sycamore Creek tumbling over the rocky riffles behind the house, and it was sometimes hard to tell its sound from a steady spring rain on the old tin roof. When it did rain, Henry would lie in contented satisfaction that everything would grow and the whole earth would be better for its freshly washed face. And the smell—Oh, what a scent came from the rain upon freshly plowed fields! . . . like nature daubing herself with perfume more exciting than Paris ever hoped to know.

Soon Henry and his family would gather at the breakfast table and sit down to Esther's famous breakfast: buckwheat cakes and sorghum molasses, fried eggs and sausage, brown bread toast or fresh aked biscuits, home-made jelly or jam, cold milk and steaming hot coffee perked until its aroma saturated everything in the house. When the lunch buckets were packed and the children were on their way to the little one-room school a mile from home, Henry would kiss Esther good-by, and, stopping at the porch to slip into his gum boots and grab his jacket and hat, he was off to the barn and the day's work.

One nice thing about Henry's day—he went to work when he wanted to; where he wanted to; when he felt like it; and when he had to. His days were determined by the sun; so having the hours pretty much certain, his days were well planned and were seldom interrupted, for there was no telephone line on Salem Pike. The nearest phone was at P. T. Wigal's General Store at Willoughby and that was seven miles of dirt road away. Mr. Wigal had a phone because he had to call to Chamberstown for merchandise, or to summon the doctor for someone on the pike, which never really did much good because the doctor always told him to tell the family to bring them to the hospital at Chamberstown and he would "check 'em over." At Whispering Pines, if Henry felt like talking to someone, he just had to talk to whoever was there; and, if he really had something to communicate to his neighbors, he just had to walk over the ridge and drop off at the head of the hollow and tell them face to face. If he had to tell someone something at Willoughby, Henry would hitch up the pair of grey mares to his road wagon and make the trip on Saturday which was his regular trading day anyway.

Esther was never too lonely. Old Brown usually lay on the back porch, and Inky the cat was constantly at the screen door, more often than not hanging on the door like a giant bat, sometimes with her claws stuck in the neat patches of wire that Esther had carefully sewn there with string. She could hear, in summer, the clicking of Henry's mowing machine in the front meadow and the buzzing of a multitude of summer insects. She often spent the morning hours tending to her roses or garden or, if in the winter, sewing on quilt patches she had promised to Hilda for her hope chest. Sometimes she just mended before the open fire, reflecting on the owner of each mended garment, and sometimes laughing over the appearance of socks without heels and pants without knees.

Then there was her kitchen—her domain—marked in every corner by the special touch of her own tastes, with its own indescribable fragrance that was a mixture of apples and spices, coffee and tea. Fresh bread mingled with the sweetness of a fresh bouquet of roses and honeysuckle, and all of it was clothed with woodsmoke. In season there was canning: beans, tomatoes, corn, beets, peaches, berries and whatever, neatly labeled and placed in the cellar house for winter. There was baking: fresh fruit pies, or pumpkin or spring rhubarb. During supper at the round table there were excited cries as eager noses sniffed her fresh hot rolls . . . their faces scrubbed with melted butter, shimmering in their lightness like dancing girls on opening night. There were corn bread and beans; when in season, new potatoes and peas creamed together; and greens from the yard with woods mushrooms as a treat; and for dessert, a pound cake that had no recipe. Often Jeff and Brent would bring home a string of bluegills or sunfish and an occasional catfish with drooping whiskers, to be rolled in meal and fried. In the fall, the Saturday hunts would yield fresh rabbit, squirrel, and even a groundhog every now and then.

Thanksgiving was butchering time . . . a baby beef or two, a pair of fat corn-fed hogs that would provide meat throughout the coming year. Who can describe the excitement of an open fire on a chilly, snow-touched Thanksgiving day, or standing watch over a boiling kettle of fat being turned into lard, while the children waited eagerly for their turn at the "cracklings" as they drifted to the top. Link sausage was made in a stuffer and seasoned just right with sage in Esther's own special way. Fresh milk, butter and eggs were always as near as the barn or the little cellar house set deep in the bank behind the house on the orchard side.

What a treasure house that cellar was in the fall! There were baskets of crisp, cool apples that waited to be peeled before the fireplace in the winter, the pears alongside, the rows and rows of canned fruits and vegetables standing in their places like glass soldiers, and a brown crock filled with fresh milk and a covered one with freshly churned butter. In the smokehouse above it, the bacons and hams all salted down wept and seeped under their penetrating coats until cured, and the popcorn hung upside down like so many yellow 'possums to add their joy to winter's confinement.

The spring house above the house always gave its clear, cold water pressed under millions of tons of hillside and purified through a half mile of rock. It was carefully caught in the spring house and piped into the kitchen; the pitcher pump at the sink gave Esther all the cold water she needed, and the saddle tanks on her wood and coal range steamed with hot water for dishes and for the wash pan on the dry sink in the corner. There was no modern plumbing in Henry's house, so the chamber pots stood guard in the bedrooms for emergencies at night, and by day the outhouse stood proudly in its place behind the chicken coop. Its whitewashed walls and welcome catalog served their purpose with a minimum of problems that mainly consisted of wasps and mud daubers, who claimed first right to the rafters. I say it served its purpose well, and even had its distinct advantages in that children didn't go as often and adults didn't stay as long; and there were almost never any plumbing problems. When there were problems, it was only every few years and then a new location solved them all in one afternoon.

Henry's family seemed to stay in good health. The only medicines and drugs they kept were aspirin, castor oil, Vicks Salve and mustard plaster (which no one liked), and Henry kept a bottle of Black Diamond Liniment on the ledge in the barn which said on the label: "Good for man or beast." It smelled like both, but seemed to work well on sprains and stiff joints. No one seemed to really know why their health was good; but the long hours they slept, the good food they ate, and the honest labor that exercised their bodies, all contributed to it. Cool, fresh milk from the cellar house was at each plate for every meal; and in the spring, Esther gave them all her special sassafras tea to "thin out their blood." They had their common ailments and miseries, and every sign of cold was treated with boiling hot lemonade, plenty of covers and a gob of Vicks. If that failed and congestion resulted, a mustard plaster was applied and the cure was, the children said, worse than the cold.

Monday was the traditional washday for Esther, and the gasoline-powered Maytag could be heard echoing off of every building on the farm for a half mile away. Henry drew the water and heated it before going to the fields on Monday, and Esther could easily do her week's wash in a half day. This was due to the fact that no one had an abundance of clothes, although each had sufficient. Henry had two or three pairs of bib overalls which he hung each night on the 40-penny spikes on his bedroom wall. When Esther washed his dirty ones, he donned a clean pair and made them last the week. When they went to Willoughby to trade on Saturdays, Henry put on a clean pair along with a fresh denim shirt. He had one good suit which he wore to church on Sunday and funerals during the week. It was the same with the children and Esther; for there didn't seem to be any particular reason to change clothes for impressing people as there just weren't too many people to impress.

Chapter IV

HENRY'S CHILDREN

The children had their tree house in a big chestnut by the creek, where they alternated between calling it a fort or a pirate ship. Sometimes it flew the Jolly Roger and other times the flag of Fort Apache; but whatever it was, it was their castle and when the rope ladder was withdrawn, they were secure from all attack. The log raft that Brent and Jeff built rode at anchor in Sycamore Creek awaiting its next Tom Sawyer and Huckleberry Finn adventure. The hole at the lower pasture was deep enough to swim in and, after Henry and the boys had spent a hot day in the hay field, Esther would often fix a lunch and meet them at the swimmin' hole for a picnic and swim. The children roamed the farm and knew every spot and named them all for future reference. They delighted in talking of these secret places in front of company, just to see their faces filled with consternation when they spoke of Dead Horse Gulch or Rim Rock Trail. There was also Crab Apple Point, Persimmon Forest, Lover's Lane, Indian Cove, Honeysuckle Jungle, Locust Ridge, or Bobcat Junction . . . each name affectionately bestowed in keeping with some peculiar characteristic of that place or some exciting thing that happened there.

In the winter beside the open fire, while green locust logs sizzled or persimmon seeped, Henry and Esther listened as the children recounted the summer's adventures at Oak Point or a horse race on the hill flat that explained why they stayed so long that day when Henry sent them after the horses. They rattled on about the rabbit box they set in the orchard and caught a chipmunk instead, and the day Brent fell out of the mulberry tree when he was supposed to be looking for the cow.

There were tea parties by Hilda with her dolls in the sideyard shade in summer with clover and honeysuckle trumpets to suck the sweetness from, or perhaps a few green apples with salt and some wild berries for dessert. On Sunday afternoons there were croquet tournaments that lasted all summer, and no one ever remembered what the actual score was. An all-summer champion was declared in the fall, with his record duly challenged for the next summer. Nobody worried too much about exercise, for one turn around the lower pasture after Daisy the cow was equivalent to five miles of jogging. One trip over "Oak Point" and its 40 acres of brush to chase and corral a stubborn calf, or an afternoon rabbit hunt, was enough exercise for anyone. For Esther, she was glad for a time during the day when she could just sit a while in the high-back country rocker and rest, while the coffee pot sang its bubbling melody and Old Brown groaned contentedly by the stove.

Winter evenings were special treats. With an apple log sizzling happily in the fire place, there were domino and checker games, chess and games on paper. There were tongue twisters, puzzles and brain teasers, as well as Indian wrestling on the floor with Henry ending up taking on all the kids at once in a free-for-all that left Esther wondering if the china cabinet would survive the crash, as Henry at last toppled to the floor like a giant with little people swarming over him like flies.

Esther would often read aloud from "Snowbound," if the snow was drifting against the house, or "Kidnapped," "Treasure Island," or the favorite of the boys, "Tom Sawyer and Huckleberry Finn." There were poems like "Little Boy Blue" that always made them cry, but best of all and long remembered were the "make-up" stories, about ghosts and monsters that roamed the Salem Pike, which were followed by the earnest question, "Did that really happen?" or "Is that really true?" Sometimes on fall nights, with a full harvest moon to light the way, they took a late night hike through the corn shocks with Hilda hanging tight to Henry's arm. Strange how, after a scary story, that cornfield, harmless in the daylight, became so foreboding as the moon cast its shadows on the neat rows of shocks and by the magic of its light turned them into hostile Indian teepees, and each pumpkin at its base seemed to be daubed with war paint as the flickering shadows played tricks on imagination and eye.

After a hot bath in the steaming water from a whistling kettle, and good-night kisses and prayers, the children marched bravely to the cold upstairs, to be lovingly tucked under heavy, home-made comforts and quilts. There in the darkness with noses chilled and imaginations running wild, every creaking board in the old farm house became a creeping ghost coming to carry them off, and the weird whispering of the pines in the front yard were sighing spirits of fallen braves, and the heavy smell of wood smoke from the fireplace downstairs the proof of their campfires.

Chapter V

HENRY'S SOCIETY

Social life was varied and sufficient. Their schedule was measured in days, not hours; and Saturday and Sunday were happy days. On Saturday, after morning chores, the grey mares were hitched to the wagon or sleigh and, when all were loaded, they moved out the lane to follow Salem Pike's carefree way to Willoughby. Brent, Jeff and Hilda soon knew every house along the seven-mile trip and each of its occupants by name. They noticed every newborn calf or colt along the way, and even noticed when Mr. Simpson replaced 13 pickets in his ailing fence. They took turns commenting on every new crop along the way and no newly painted building, litter of puppies, fresh cow or weedy garden escaped their notice. They also kept a running tally of groundhog holes along the road, wren's nests, snakes, rabbits, toads, turtles, woolly worms and chipmunks. The boys always took a turn at driving those proud grey mares, and while one gee'd and haw'd, the other pretended he was riding shotgun on the Pony Express to Abilene. Henry and Esther talked of the things they would buy at Wigal's and the people they would meet.

While Henry loaded the feed, wire and hardware items, Esther took her eggs and cream to trade with Mr. Wigal for the kind of things men couldn't understánd . . . thread, binding, staples, lye, and always at the end of trading a poke (as Mr. Wigal always called it) of pink lozenges or black sticky licorice for the kids. Sometimes they bought overalls for the boys and Henry, and new dresses for Esther and Hilda.

Henry liked to sit outside on the porch of the store in the sun and talk, or drift to the field across the road where a perpetual horseshoe game was carried on. No one seldom threw less than double ringers, so they were exciting as were the softball games that seemed to materialize, like clouds of a summer storm, out of nowhere. Usually they ended up being played between the old men and the young men and, when they were over, the men were red-faced and panting and the boys sweaty and victorious.

Saturday nights often saw socials sponsored by the M. E. Church or by the Farm Women's Club, at which time there was homemade vegetable soup, ice cream and pop in tubs of ice, candy and fresh baked cakes and pies to be sold and consumed. Then there were other times, when there was visiting at the neighbors with the adults sitting on the porch talking and laughing, and the kids sneaking around listening and laughing at the old folks or mocking them to the happy giggling of those they wanted to impress. There was hide-and-seek in the yard or hiding games in the hay mow with the old folks always worried about them falling out, which they seldom ever did, and when they did no one ever told. These wonderful times saw budding romances that became the topics of whispered and giggled conferences for weeks between the children.

Sundays there was church morning and evening, with the afternoons for visiting and games. The mingling of the young people before these meetings was a special time, and occasionally the permission to walk home together along Salem Pike in the moonlight was a treat long remembered. Their shouts and laughter filled the evening air, and life somehow seemed good and full of promise. Once or twice a year a protracted meeting saw meetings every night, and many visitors from Willoughby making the trip by wagon and an occasional four-wheeled Jeep.

Summertime had its share of family reunions at which time everyone ate too much, talked too long and got sunburned playing softball or pitching horseshoes. There was the annual Willoughby homecoming with its speeches, ice cream turned on the grounds, fried chicken, pie, cake and the annual sermon by the town minister. Best of all was the long wagon ride home from Simpson's grove amid the fragrance of fresh mown clover; and while the children fell into exhausted sleep, Henry and Esther sat together behind the plodding team and dreamed, talked, loved and lived.

When serious illness or death came to Salem Pike, there was that strange fellowship of neighbors that seemed to fill the house with baked goods and to rally to a hayfield that needed to be put up, or a woodshed that needed to be filled. No one seemed to organize it—it just seemed to organize itself. Folks just did naturally what naturally had to be done. There were fumbling expressions of sympathy that never seemed to be adequate; but when it was over, the bereaved and the needy knew that someone cared and were concerned and that somehow, they were not alone.

Henry and Esther never seemed to accumulate any great amount of money; but when a cow was fresh, or a calf big enough to veal, or the chickens laid well, there was enough for the extra needs and even some to put away for that "rainy day" everyone expects in life. Henry liked to tell Esther that they had everything they needed, and with food and raiment and shelter they had found the true secret of contentment, as the Bible says. Henry, on their long walks through the fields on a Sunday afternoon, would remind Esther how God's word says that godliness with contentment was great gain and that by this standard they had gained a lot. They had a little money saved and felt they could always manage if "something happened," for Henry remembered his father saying often, "Where there is a will, there is a way."

Henry would talk often of the day when Brent and Jeff would take over the farm when he was not able, and he could sit on the porch in the same rocking chair his father had rocked in while Henry worked the farm. Jokingly, Henry told Esther that he was looking forward to that, so he could boss a little the way his dad had done. "Whispering Pines will never change," he often said, "and the life we have known here will never change, unless *we* change.

One spring morning, when he had persuaded Esther to walk over the hill with him to see about a new calf, he took her by the hand and together they walked to a favorite hill of Henry's. There, with the wind blowing lightly through Esther's hair, they could see the length of Salem Pike and the whole valley with its green and brown fields stretched before them. They sat beneath the towering pines on that point Henry had named "Shiloh"; for, he explained, it means "rest." The wind sighed in the branches of the trees as though in prayer; and Henry hallowed that spot by obtaining the pledge from Esther that when he was gone she would bring him to Shiloh, and there beneath the pines, overlooking his beloved valley, he could rest from a life well lived. When Esther said he was too somber, he kissed her and holding her close said, "That time is a long way off. We have this moment to love and live and nothing can change that. I remember the lines of that poem by Robert Frost which I love to read before the fire. Shall I quote it for you?" And then looking deep into her eyes, he said:

"The woods are lovely, dark and deep
But I have promises to keep
And miles to go before I sleep."

The rushing wind through the pines seemed now to groan as though the words of Henry's poem had become a prophecy of things to come.

Chapter VI
PROGRESS COMES TO WILLOUGHBY

It was inevitable that the progress of Chamberstown should spill out of its overflowing cup into Willoughby. The 30 miles of gravel from Chamberstown had been replaced with smooth blacktop and with that improvement came a marked increase in activity in Willoughby. The trains still made their scheduled runs, for no progress can discourage them from their appointed rounds—but other things had changed. For one thing, almost no one gathered at P. T. Wigal's to see the "Cannonball" go through, although many times the store was filled with shoppers. It might have had to do with the change in the store itself. The old ball field across the road had been paved to make way for a new parking lot which Mr. Wigal said was needed, for the new blacktop from Chamberstown had brought a lot of folk to Willoughby who wanted to "get out of town a little." Mr. Simpson's grove was the first to feel the iron fist of progress. When a man from town offered him $750 for an acre lot to build a house, Mr. Simpson rightly concluded that he couldn't afford to keep a picnic grove for the good of the community when the lot was worth such a price as that. So before long Mr. Simpson's house sported a new TV tower and a color TV, and Simpson's Shady Grove development was a reality. Soon others from town had joined the first pioneer and, at last account, the lots were selling for as much as $1500 each and only a few were left. I need not add that this greatly inspired others to join the boom and soon Willoughby was no longer a sleepy little country community, but a thriving, progressive, bustling rural center.

Mr. Wigal began to feel the backlash of community prosperity and was forced to remodel the interior of his store. Henry was in there after the changes were made, and it seemed funny not to see P. T. Wigal there to greet him with a handclasp and a friendly smile. One of the carry-out boys explained that Mr. Wigal spent his time in the balcony office that overlooked the new Wigal Super Market, for there was an awful lot of book work to take care of now. Henry could see the shiny file cabinets full of records and wondered what happened to the old single-book ledger Mr. Wigal used to pull out from under the counter to jot down the trading transactions.

Henry couldn't deny that the self-service idea was novel, and the checkout counters surely seemed to make things move faster. Although he and Esther could now shop easier and quicker, somehow it seemed a little eerie that there was no one gathered on the porch to trade knives and small talk. The old wooden porch with its gloriously carved-by-hand benches, where Henry had first sat as a boy to listen to his father talk, had been removed. Mr. Wigal said he didn't want to encourage loitering in front of the store because the city people that had moved to Willoughby were in a hurry to get their shopping done.

Of course, Mr. Wigal gave up gardening behind the store. He had to—the drive-through car wash bought his garden spot for $2,000 and, as he said, "You can sure buy a lot of beans and 'taters for that kind of money!" Nobody could argue with that kind of logic. Widow Abbot still came there to trade, or I should say "shop" because she learned that her eggs couldn't be traded any more for groceries; but she was informed that there was still a place in Chamberstown that would take them. (She never found a way to get them there.) As I said, she still shopped there but was a little perplexed and a little frightened at the way things were. Mr. Wigal used to know where everything was placed in the store, but nobody seemed to know now; and she kind of missed Mr. Wigal's inquiry about her health. I guess the inquiry and the opportunity it afforded to unburden herself from time to time was one of the main reasons she came daily to Wigal's store. Henry said recently that he heard she had taken to her bed and wasn't expected to live too long.

The thing most people hated to see go was the old Burnside stove. It had been sort of the "town hall" of Willoughby for 75 years. There had been many a village problem solved around its cherry-red sides. It was still around, but it was at present delegated to a place in Wigal's warehouse behind the compressors for his fancy meat and produce cases. A new service station had replaced the single gas pump that had stood at Wigal's for years, and the people of Willoughby sure were getting things fixed up nice and convenient.

Henry always seemed glad to get back to Whispering Pines where there was peace and quiet. His trips to Willoughby didn't come as often, nor last as long, and he seemed a little reluctant to talk about it. Esther guessed that it had to do with the time the grey mares were scared bad by some teenage boys showing off in their sports car in front of the store. Hilda thought it had more to do with the remarks the boys made about Henry being an "old farmer" and the embarassed look on Jeff and Brent's faces as they rode into Willoughby in their wagon.

Chapter VII

GOOD THINGS COME TO HENRY

The progress that had begun to change the face of Willoughby soon slithered out Salem Pike in the form of a visit to Whispering Pines by three of Henry's neighbors. After wiping their feet at the door and being invited into Esther's sweet-smelling kitchen, they were dutifully seated at the round table for coffee. They seemed rather embarrassed and after chit-chat about the crops, Mr. Danner pulled out a legal looking paper and said in a funny voice, "Well, Henry, just as well get down to business. This here's a petition. Clayton Peters' idea was that with all the new tax revenue the county's got, due to the new plant at Chamberstown, and the way Willoughby's booming, it sure looked like the right time to press 'em for improving Salem Pike." Ed Stevens added his enthusiasm, "You know, Henry, Salem Pike being widened and gravelled, or blacktopped, would cut eight miles off the trip from Willoughby to Chamberstown. Not only that, but we've been talkin', Henry, and Salem Pike would become the through route to the county seat and that's goin' to bring a lot of prosperity to all of us. Why—if lots at Willoughby are goin' for $1500, think what your upper meadow would be worth before long if that road opened up!"

Henry had a troubled look on his serious face; and slowly, with the feeling that no one was going to hear him, he said, "But, Ed, I don't want to sell my upper meadow. That's the best piece of hay ground in this valley. My mares know every inch of that field and somehow it don't seem right that bulldozers and strangers should tear it up."

Charlie Moore spoke up, "I know how you feel, Henry, but this thing means a lot to all of us and you know, you can't fight progress. It's gonna come and you'll see—it'll be good for all of us. Think what that extra money could mean to you and Esther and the kids! No more grubbin' in the ground to make out . . . ." Somehow Henry had never thought of his life as "grubbin' in the ground to make out"; it had seemed to him to be a good life and his by choice. He looked at Esther, his eyes pleading for her advice; but she looked away and soon got up to fetch more coffee. Fred Danner said, "Esther, what do you think about it?" For a while she just fussed with the stove, and at last in a quiet voice she said, "Whatever Henry thinks is best about it is all right with me." Henry cleared his husky voice and promised, "We'll talk about it and let you know. How soon does something have to be done?" "Two weeks," Ed Stevens replied and then added in a pleading tone—"And remember, Henry, a lot depends on your signature. All the commissioners think highly of you and your father. You got a good name in this county and your opinion will carry a lot of weight. I'd hate to think you'd use that influence to keep the rest of us from the *good things in life.*" With the usual thanks to Esther for her hospitality and the small talk of people saying good-by, the meeting adjourned as abruptly as it had convened and soon Henry and Esther were alone in the kitchen.

In the two weeks that followed, Henry was deep in thought about the petition. The phrase "the good things in life" bothered him a lot. One day he came in from the barn and blurted out—"Esther, I got to know somethin'. Do you and the children feel that you are being deprived of the *good things in life?*" Esther looked hurt and putting her arms around his solid shoulders said, "Henry, I've never felt that we have missed anything in life. We have each other, and as long as that's true, we'll never lack for anything. I've been thinking too, Henry. Maybe we should sign for the benefit of the others. Nothing can change *our* lives. Whispering Pines will always be the same, just as it was with your father and grandfather. They moved with the times and nothing happened. Let them build their road. Like I said, Henry, as long as we have each other, nothing can change us." Henry kissed her on the end of her nose, like he always did when he was preoccupied, and hurried out to the barn.

The next day, as Henry was trying to get Daisy in the barn lot, Ed Stevens' wagon drove in the lane and with him were Charlie Moore and Fred Danner. Henry hurried to the house to meet them and walked into the kitchen in time to hear Esther saying, "It's like I told Henry, Fred, there's nothing to fear in progress. It can only change those who want to be changed. We don't want to keep anybody from the *good things in life*." It was that phrase again that seemed to trouble Henry. It seemed to eat away at the security he had always felt in his way of life. He had never felt he had to take a back seat to anyone. He felt confident that he had given his children the best heritage life had to offer. Now—he wasn't so sure. All this talk about the good things in life and prosperity, and money making them possible, disturbed him; but like Esther said, it didn't seem like anything could change unless they changed—and Henry was determined that would never happen.

After the usual formalities of greeting, Fred said, "Well, Henry, you know why we're here. We got to turn this petition over to Mr. Wigal who has promised to take it to the meeting of the commissioners on Friday. And you ought to know this—he said it was a sure thing if you signed it. You know they got the influence of the post office department behind it too; for it means Clayton Peters can sell that old horse and get him a car to carry the rural route." Henry thought of Old Ted and wondered what he would do out in pasture all day and if he would miss the sugar hand-outs along the route. It seemed like that change in Clayton's life would be a good one, but the mail would never be the same without Old Ted.

Henry said quickly, "I'm goin' to sign; not because I want to, but it sure don't seem right that I should do anything that would keep you people from the *good things in life.*" Now he found that he had used that phrase himself, and the more he heard it and used it the more it seemed like maybe there *was* something he had missed. "Well", thought Henry, "we'll see." He picked up the pen offered by Charlie Moore and signed—"Henry L. Morgan," and underneath Esther in her fine hand wrote "Esther A. Morgan," and it was done. They shook hands all around, and with much light conversation the men made their way to the lane where their wagon and team stood patiently by.

As Ed Stevens picked up the lines to turn his wagon around, he said with a grin, "Take a good look at this old rig, Henry; for if this thing goes through, I'll be cruisin' down that big road in a new car. I've already got a standing offer for the corner of my big meadow, you know where those big red oaks stand." Henry couldn't think of anything to say and they drove out with the creaking and rattling of the wagon mingling with the excited talk of the three men. As they disappeared in the turn in Salem Pike, Henry thought about those red oaks of Ed's. Grandpa Morgan used to tell him that old Chief Tecumseh himself used to camp there when the Shawnee had hunted the valley, and it must have been true, because Henry still had the arrowheads he found there when he was a boy. He wondered what the bulldozers would do to it all and what Chief Tecumseh would think if he could see the progress that was coming to Salem Pike.

Chapter VIII

HENRY'S WORLD ENLARGES

The road was hastily approved and soon men and equipment were swarming all up and down the pike. The commissioners visited the scene themselves with the county engineers, and the right-of-way was secured from all involved parties. It upset Henry because when the 40 foot right-of-way was staked off, it took out the big mulberry tree in the corner of his barn lot; and he had to move his fence in places; and somehow it irritated him to think of strangers defiling the sanctity of Salem Pike. But he remembered what Charlie had said about not being able to fight progress; so he just busied himself in the back meadow plowing and discing and pretended like nothing was happening. But it was.

Several months later the dust had settled; the dozers and trucks were removed; the last red-flagged stakes pulled up, final inspections made, and Salem Pike had somehow been transformed into a 30 foot blacktop with a shiny white line down the middle. The commissioners had been real considerate and placed a "cattle crossing" sign at the barn lot, but in the days ahead nobody seemed to pay too much attention to it. Soon the traffic from Chamberstown to Willoughby zoomed by Whispering Pines at 60 miles per hour, and Henry never realized how many people he and Esther seemed to know, for almost every one of them blew their horn in passing. Not many of them stopped, and when they did it was to say that they had just been driving by and stopped to say "Hello," which they did and then drove on. Henry and Esther were amazed at how many people had so many places to go and so many things to do. They noted that often they saw the same car making two and three trips a day to Willoughby or to Chamberstown and marveled at how complex their lives must be to require so much business in the city.

Nothing changed in the Morgans' lives at once. Nothing, that is, until the second trip to Willoughby on Saturday to do their shopping. That was the day the mares bolted into the ditch when the tractor-trailer came too close and the wagon nearly upset. Henry did get upset and shouted things he shouldn't have at the driver. Of course, he could hardly hear him, or care, for by that time he was two miles down the pike. When Henry came home that day he told Esther that he just couldn't take the team to town anymore. Not only was it dangerous to get out on the highway, but he couldn't stand the remarks and the embarrassment to the children when they came in the wagon to Wigal's. Henry had seen Fred Danner at the store that day, and Fred said he would be glad to stop by for Henry any Saturday he wanted to come to town, and that seemed to be the answer. The following weeks Henry rode to Willoughby with Fred and all went well until he overheard a remark at the post office about people that imposed on their neighbors when they could have their own car as well as the next man. This troubled Henry and Esther, for they had never been people to impose on anyone; and if it worked a hardship on Fred that they didn't know about, well—there was but one thing to do and that was to see about a car.

Henry got a ride to Chamberstown with Ed Stevens the following Tuesday, the day he had set aside to cultivate the cornfield. While Ed tended to his business at the court house, Henry looked over the used cars. He was shocked at the prices they asked and learned that the cars carried no guarantee or warranty of any kind. He learned a new phrase that all of them used, "As is." He came home discouraged and told Esther that a used car would wipe out his savings; for any car that would be decent would cost $1,000 and that was almost the exact amount of what he had saved for a rainy day. "Well," he joked, "maybe this is the rainy day we've been expecting; but to tell you the truth, I never expected such a storm."

The following Monday, the day he thought sure he would get the big meadow mowed, he and Esther went to Chamberstown to see about the car. Henry said he thought if they rode in with Mr. Wigal, who always went there early on Monday to see about merchandise, they could be back by noon. So they arrived and were taken in tow by a friendly used-car salesman, who soon fixed them up with a "real sharp" four-year-old car that was a one-owner, local driver car, "good as new and would give years of trouble-free service," he said. This relieved Henry considerably; for the thought of any repairs or further expense frightened him. The deal almost fell through when Henry told the man that $1,000 was all the money he had, and the man told him that there was an additional $55 for taxes, license and title transfer. Henry hadn't thought of that, and the man had failed to tell him that part the time before. So, after calling the manager, there was further kindness shown to Henry by the good manager agreeing to "knock off" $55 from the price as a personal favor to Henry. This unexpected kindness impressed Henry and as he later told Esther, "It sure proved the honesty of those people."

Since the car was automatic, there was nothing in learning how to operate it and, after a visit to the court house, Henry obtained a learner's permit and off he and Esther went in a cloud of exhaust (just like Ed Stevens said he would do, "cruisin' down the big road" in their new car). Henry had to admit it gave him a sense of power as he cruised down the highway toward Whispering Pines. They thought it would be a good surprise to drop by the school and pick up the kids on the way home. As they pulled in the school yard, a sense of pride swept over Henry as the kids admired the car and showed it to their friends.

He was consoled as they drove homeward and he heard the excited chatter of the children in the back seat planning all the places they could go now, and Henry wondered if maybe this wasn't one of the good things in life he had heard so much about.

Chapter IX

HENRY IS ENLIGHTENED

Things didn't change too much for Henry; at least it didn't seem like they changed a whole lot. He noticed that their trips to Willoughby were more frequent than ever before and that instead of once a week, on Saturday, they were going three and four times a week, sometimes with the children and sometimes without them. And it didn't really matter; Willoughby was no longer a treat to any of them, and necessity dictated the frequency of their trips. Henry did notice that when the family went to Willoughby, there wasn't time to see anything along the way, and the children usually talked in the back seat or read comic books they got at Wigal's new magazine rack.

He wondered if the children had forgotten how many groundhog holes there were in the seven miles to Willoughby; but then remembered that you couldn't see woolly worms, turtles, groundhogs, snakes, toads, rabbits, fences, barns, houses, or people very well at 60 miles per hour. There wasn't even too much time to think along the way, for eight or nine minutes didn't give you too much time to think; and what with the billboards spewing out their messages at you as you went by, and the road signs to watch—well, that's how it was. Anyway the kids always wanted the radio on when they were riding in the car. That way they could hear the latest music, which Henry didn't understand, nor want to, and Esther could hear the commercials about all the things that went on in Chamberstown. The influence of these commercials sure did make themselves felt; for every now and then Esther would say, "Henry, could we drive over to Chamberstown tomorrow to the sale?" and then would follow a glowing account of the many bargains offered at the new Seers department store in the county seat. When objecting that they could not afford to buy the things offered, he was met with the irresistible argument that the time to buy these things is not when you need them, but when you can buy them at a great savings.

One night at the Seers store, Esther was just "looking around" while Henry looked at his pocket watch. She discovered a "fantastic" bargain in clothing for the whole family, and he complained he should be home in bed because a full day tomorrow hauling hay would demand all the strength he could muster. Henry objected that they simply didn't have the money and anyway his old overalls were good enough. Esther replied that it wouldn't hurt him to have some sport shirts and slacks and look "a little decent" when they came to town. This hurt Henry, but he looked at himself and then at the other men around him, and he wished he were back at Whispering Pines and up on that point that overlooked the valley. No one could see his overalls there. He conceded that she was right; then the clerk assured Henry that it would only take "a minute" to open an easy-payment account, and then they could buy anything they wanted with just a minimum of trouble.

Now Henry had never heard of the "easy-payment" plan. The only kind of payment he knew anything about was cash. Oh, he remembered how once or twice when things were real bad that his dad had gone to the bank and got a 90-day note for a small amount to "tide them over," as Dad used to say. The bank president was a personal friend of Henry's dad, and it was more of a favor than a business transaction. The banker even flushed at having to ask for a signature, for he had always said that Frank Morgan's word was as good as his bond. Henry had always looked upon borrowing as an emergency measure at the very best, and the thought of borrowing to buy clothes he didn't feel he needed, was strange.

This was soon overcome by the credit manager turning out to be an old schoolmate of Henry's who had long since gone to Chamberstown to make his fortune. He assured Henry that "everybody" has an easy-payment account at Seers, and that the convenience of it was something no one could afford to be without. Being known to the credit manager won Henry quick temporary approval and he soon left the office clutching his key to the *good things of life*—a credit card. They soon made their purchase, and on the way home they talked about how easy it was to buy now and pay later. Of course, neither of them realized that they had only "bought now"; for the "pay later" had not yet manifested itself for what it was. Anyway, he had 45 days until a payment was due and in 45 days many things could happen. And they did.

A few days later Henry was summoned to the house to talk to a man from the power company, who drove an orange Jeep into Henry's lane. The man came quickly to the point. The improved highway had forced the power company to match the progress of the community and a transmission line from Willoughby up the Salem Pike would soon be a reality. Henry said that was all right with him, for he could not see how a transmission line had anything to do with him. But it did.

He was told that the other neighbors were already signed up for electric service and that electricity would open up a whole new dimension to living. He would soon know the joys of living better electrically. Again he was assured that the good things of life would come by the harnessing of this powerful giant in his home.

Esther was thrilled at the prospect; for already she and the children had been fascinated with the many, many electrical appliances on sale at Seers. Henry mildly objected that there was no wiring in his house, nor had there been for 75 years, and that to wire his house would be a tremendous expense which he could not afford. The kind man from the power company said they had a provision that would overcome the difficulty. A ten-year deferred payment plan and their own sub-contractors would take care of all the details. Henry asked if this was like Seers Easy-Payment Plan, and was assured that it was even easier than that.

The estimated cost of Henry's house wiring would come to $1500 and spread over ten years with 7% interest would be only $20.80 per month; a negligible amount indeed for such a whole new world of easy living. What the man didn't tell Henry was that besides the $1500 initial cost, over the ten years he would pay $1050 in interest, thereby almost doubling the cost of it all. When Henry asked how much the interest would amount to, he was put at ease by being told he didn't have to worry about it; for any time he chose, he could pay it all off and owe only for the time he had the loan.

It was all bewildering at first, but the more he thought about it, the simpler it became; and the man said the contractors could begin the first of the week and that by the time the transmission line, now under construction, was finished, Henry could be enjoying the blessings of electricity. Henry said reluctantly to Esther, "If this is what you and the kids want, it's all right with me. I don't want you to be without the good things in life as long as I can provide them." The man was pleased and the contracts were drawn up and Henry wrote laboriously, "Henry L. Morgan" on the proper line and Esther in her fine hand wrote, "Esther A. Morgan" on the line beneath. And so began the fascinating world of electric appliance magic.

Chapter X

HENRY CHANGES

Henry noticed that he kept getting farther and farther behind in his work due to the many interruptions and involvements of late. There was a time when getting behind didn't bother him too much, for there was no set schedule to keep. Like the spring he wasn't feeling too well and decided he just wouldn't plow the south 40 at all, and so he just laid it by for the season and so reduced his work schedule for the summer months. That was not as easy now, for the pressure of those two payment books began to prey upon Henry's mind. Frustration began to slip into Henry's day and instead of the freedom he once felt in the field, he now began to feel that he was there because he *had* to be, sick or well. He made himself a solemn promise to get out from under those obligations as quickly as he could and then, he assured himself, all would be like it was. He thought as he walked round and round behind the mares how soon he could pay the power company off and then slip back to a normal life again. That was before the insurance man called on him.

He hated leaving the field just as he was getting things under way so well; but the insurance man couldn't come back at night and he assured Esther, who came to the field for Henry, that their happiness and peace of mind depended upon seeing him. Henry came to the house a little irritated at being interrupted in the middle of a work day, but the man soon soothed his irritation by telling him the latest accident figures in Mindoah County and what the percentages were of he and Esther being killed in a head-on collision and, for the good of his family and for the protection of society at large, Henry must in all haste insure himself, his auto, and their home against accident and loss or death.

The man hinted that the state would eventually require him to have auto insurance or park his car and, when Henry thought of the $1,000 savings he had sunk into that car, he remembered about the battle being lost for the want of a horse, etc. The papers were quickly, but not painlessly, drawn up and he begrudgingly signed, "Henry L. Morgan" on the appropriate line and Esther in her fine hand signed, "Esther A. Morgan" on the line beneath.

Relieved that he was at last in the quiet of his field and away from the reach of further interruption, Henry consoled himself with the thought that the monthly payment on the total house, car and $10,000 life insurance policies was only $24.70. Mentally calculating his total obligation at $55.50 per month, Henry realized that he would have to part with at least one cow from his small herd of white-face cattle he had slowly built up over the years. All of this agitated him a little. The next morning after breakfast, when he should have finished the field he had left undone because of yesterday's interruption, Henry hired Bill Baxter to haul one of the cattle to the sale where she brought a handsome amount. With the money from the cow sale, he was able to pay the Seers account to a minimum, and with the remainder he made a substantial payment to the power company.

That night after supper as Esther lit the lamps, she told Henry that after tomorrow the old lamps would be finished forever, and she was glad. The contractors had finished and in the morning the power company was to hook up Henry's house to the new black pole that stood in the barn lot. This filled Henry's heart with mixed emotions, but everyone else seemed so happy about it that he soon forgot it in the fun that followed.

They gathered in the living room and the checkers and dominoes were brought out, and soon Henry realized that Whispering Pines hadn't changed much after all and that the good things in life had helped. He begged off from the story-time saying he was more tired than usual, and he explained that all the running and confusion had worn him out a little. So shortening the evening as graciously as he could, he soon fell in bed convinced that it was as Esther said, "Nothing will change unless we change"; and Henry was sure that would never happen.

As he lay there in the darkness wondering why he couldn't drop off to sleep as he once did, he suddenly realized with panic that something was wrong! He awakened Esther and said, "What's wrong?" She sleepily replied, "There's nothing wrong. Go to sleep. It'll be a long day tomorrow." He was sure of this, but the uneasiness wouldn't go away. In the darkness he suddenly knew what was wrong—things *had* changed. He couldn't hear the whippoorwill any more. The silence had no more soothing effect, for there was no more silence. He could hear the roar of the late traffic as it went by the house and every now and then the squeal of tires as teenagers "laid rubber," as they called it, on the straight stretch from Henry's barn to the turn at Fred Danner's lane. He noticed that the smell of honeysuckle no longer drifted through the bedroom window, for the window was now shut to keep the exhaust fumes from entering. Even if the window had been open, Henry couldn't have smelled the honeysuckle for the county engineer had ordered it all sprayed to kill it. Henry hadn't known before that it was a "nuisance weed" and would soon "take over the county" if it wasn't stamped out. In the darkness Henry thought of Old Brown and how he tried to make it from the barn to the house a few weeks ago and hadn't heard the engine whine of the car that killed him. Old Brown had never had to look out for anybody before, and he hadn't realized that when progress comes, no one looks out for *you*.

Henry also wondered why there hadn't been any socials for a long time like there used to be, and all of a sudden he got sick. Not physically, although he could feel this sickness from his heart to his stomach; it was a homesickness that crept over him in the darkness . . . homesickness for the life that seemed to be slipping away in the changes that came while everybody said nothing was changing. The attendance at the socials had so dropped off after the road improvement, and with everyone having so many places to go and things to do, that they had slipped into oblivion. Church attendance had dropped off and protracted meetings just couldn't draw out the people like they once did. He heard the clock in the living room strike 12:00 and panicked at the thought of working a full day in the field tomorrow with a short night's rest. He promised himself that tomorrow he would surely talk to Esther about the unwelcome changes in their life. He planned to take this matter up with her at the lunch table tomorrow.

Chapter XI

HENRY MEETS THE GREAT SOCIETY

At the lunch table the next day, Henry heard from Esther how the big orange trucks had come right after he went to the barn and the men hooked up the shiny wires at the pole to the entrance cable, now proudly tied to Henry's house. At last the wonderful world of electricity was theirs and all the magic of its power was at the flick of a switch—before Henry realized that all the power in the world could not light an empty socket. They laughed at their stupidity in forgetting to buy bulbs for the light fixtures, and Henry agreed to run to town right after dark and get a few.

This was all changed by an orange car in the lane and the well-dressed man with the brief case and package under his arm. Introducing himself as the salesman from the appliance division of the power company, he presented Henry with a sample package of light bulbs, and the glory of electric power came to Whispering Pines. Screwing in the bulbs, Henry was fascinated with the ease with which he could flood the house with light. No wicks to trim, no chimneys to wash and no danger of fire—that is, not too much danger. "You will be billed every 10th day of the month for around $10. But the amount depends on you," the salesman explained. He hastily added that there were other pressing matters he had to talk over—such as a farm light for the barnyard at a mere $4.50 per month. He explained about thieves being afraid of night lights and how convenient it would be at night to have a work light where Henry could catch up on things around the barn. All this seemed right and reasonable and the light was ordered. Henry thought ahead and realized that now with lights at his disposal he was no longer limited to sunup to sunset as he and his father had been, but now all the chores could be done after dark and he would have more time in his fields. This brought a whole new dimension to Whispering Pines. Now a 24-hour day was within reach and things would surely smooth out in Henry's troubled life.

Then the man brought out the appliance catalog and began to tell Henry how the genius of electric power lay in the many, many time and labor-saving devices available to them. The glories of each were properly extolled, and Henry and Esther's eyes reflected the wonder that filled and fired their imaginations. Who could imagine an electric-powered plumbing system with their very own bathroom in the house itself! No more cold trips to the outhouse! No more chamber pots to empty! The convenience — the santitation — the comfort — the security of it all overwhelmed them; and Henry heard himself saying in a strange voice, "How much would the payments be on a whole plumbing system?" The man explained that this was for a plumbing contractor to figure, but he would surely send him around the next day. Henry had hoped to get the barn cleaned out then, but this was important too, he reasoned.

The good things of life were coming fast and furious, and before the electric man left that day, Henry found himself signing in a bold hand, "Henry L. Morgan" on the appropriate line and Esther in her fine hand wrote, "Esther A. Morgan" on the line under his name. The list was impressive—a toaster to make instant toast, an iron to help Esther have more time around the house, an electric sewing machine, two radios (one for the kitchen and one for the barn; it makes the cows easier to milk according to scientific studies), three electric clocks, seven lamps (although they had lived for years with four oil lamps), an electric heating system, a wonderful electric range, a large refrigerator, automatic washer and clothes dryer, a 22 foot deep freeze, and last, but not least in the eyes of the children, a 24 inch black and white TV and as a bonus a free 40 foot tower that would even "pull in Columbia and Dexter City."

The grand total was $3,021.43 and the best part of all—it could be spread over five years with no payments for 45 days, and the payments were only $50.34 per month. This brought Henry's total obligaton to the fantastic sum of $120.64 per month. This was actually more money than he had seen many times in three months. That night after Esther had dropped off to sleep, dreaming of the wonderful world of time and labor-saving devices that would arrive the next day, Henry realized that his problems had only begun. Where would he put all these things? The toaster and iron were no problem, and a place for the radios and lamps would be no problem; but the deep freeze, dryer, washer and furnace troubled him considerably. It was after the clock had struck 2:00 A.M. that Henry had finally devised a plan and fell exhausted into a short night's sleep.

Morning came quickly and Henry didn't spring out of bed as he usually did. He could hardly drag and guessed he would shake it off in a little fresh air. He just had to get that barn cleaned, but the plumbing contractor was to be here this morning and the barn would have to wait. After all, Esther reminded him, the barn lights were now working and he could do that after supper and maybe the children would want to help him. It would be like old times again, with them helping and perhaps some time to play in the hay mow or tell a story. It might not be as good under the electric lights as it once was under the oil lamps, but they would make out. "No sir," Henry assured himself, "nothing will change unless *I* change—and I'm not going to change!"

The plumbing man came right on schedule and got down to business at once. The electric man had called him at home the night before and he had a plumbing system all worked out for Henry. To install bathroom, laundry facilities, new kitchen sink, drill a well and install the pump, all parts and labor came to the modest sum of $1,967.93. This seemed to stagger Henry for a moment, as he was not quite recovered from the appliance salesman's visit of the day before. He was bolstered by the plan he had worked out during the night and told the salesman that he would have to do some arranging before he could obligate himself for such additional payments. The plumbing man assured him that they wished to work no hardship on him and they could install the system now and no payments for six months, if he wished. Henry stalled him by promising to buy the package, but he would work out his own financial arrangements. The man left after making an appointment for Saturday morning. This was the day Henry had hoped to vaccinate the cattle.

Henry told Esther he would be gone for the remainder of the day and to tell the children when they came from school not to plan anything for he wanted them to start on the barn as soon as school was out. He had forgotten that the appliances were beginning to arrive and that by 3:00 that afternoon the TV would be connected.

He hurried to the barn and, getting into his "sharp" used car, he drove with determination to Chamberstown and striding into the First National Bank asked for Will Jenkins, a personal friend of his father and a friend of Henry's for years. Will was up in years, and they had delegated him to an office in the rear, although he was still the president of the bank. The young board of directors felt that Will's ideas were old-fashioned and they were only waiting for him to die. He was delighted to see Henry and, after trivialities, Henry stated his case as briefly as he could; he wanted to take a mortgage on Whispering Pines. He thought that if he could borrow about $7500 on the place over a period of 20 years he could handle it very nicely. That would enable him to pay off the power company, the appliance contract, buy the plumbing package and leave him with about $1,000 to enclose the long back porch for a place for his new freezer, washer and dryer.

This seemed reasonable to Will, though at first he was shocked at the thought of mortgaging Whispering Pines, and he reminded Henry that to his knowledge the farm had never been mortgaged. He said some other things; among them, that he hoped Henry knew what he was doing and Henry said he was sure he did. Then he explained to Will how you can't fight progress and that he wouldn't want to deny his family any of the good things in life. Will agreed and, with a word to the loan officer, the papers were filled out and Henry signed "Henry L. Morgan" on the appropriate line and left a line blank for Esther's signature. He made a fast trip to Whispering Pines and soon Esther had written, "Esther A. Morgan" in her fine little hand in the blank space, and Henry was on his way back to the bank. Everything went smoothly and, with the $7500 deposited in a new checking account, he went home relieved that for only $55 per month he had wiped out those giant debts, had enough to buy the plumbing the family wanted so badly and extra money to enclose the porch.

The next few days saw a flurry of excitement at Whispering Pines. The porch was enclosed; the old iron, sewing machine, oil lamps, washer and kitchen range were all neatly piled in the smokehouse, none of which they would ever need again—thank goodness! The furnace was installed in a neat corner of the new room on the porch and the washer, dryer and deep freeze stood at attention in their places like robots waiting the beck and call of their master. Esther dreamed of the additional time and energy she would now have with all the time and labor-saving devices at the flick of her fingers. The old spring was permanently abandoned as a health hazard, and the new pump purred contentedly in its place. The new bathroom glistened with sanitation and was warm with comfort and invited all to its convenience.

Now the effect of all this on Henry was readily seen. He was nervous and irritable and each night found him retiring later and later. Trying to keep up with the farm and with all this progress was wearing poor Henry out. The long evenings before the fire were history, and he realized that there had been no communication among the members of his family for weeks; no, not even for months. The evenings were saved, however, by the presence of TV which proved to be one of the good things in life for Henry. It saved him the responsibility of listening to the stupid questions of Jeff, Brent and Hilda and the weary task of trying with a tired mind to think up one of those ridiculous stories he used to tell. He wondered why they hadn't discovered the cure-all for family problems—TV—a long time ago. As far as reading was concerned, the books had long since been sent to the attic to make room for the TV; and he noticed that the tree house was rotting down, and the raft that Jeff and Brent had so laboriously built had sunk in the last spring rains and nobody noticed.

He swore again that Whispering Pines would once more be as it was, but he was too tired to think of any way to bring it to pass. The good old days, when he was deprived of the good things of life, seemed like a dream. For the first time in his life, spring had come and gone and the garden was never plowed and as a result there was not a single can put in the cellar that year. Esther consoled him by saying nobody could raise and can beans, tomatoes, etc. as cheaply as you could buy them on sale at the super market. Butchering seemed like a waste of time when good ground beef could be purchased for 59¢ a pound and sometimes cheaper. Henry tried to tell Esther that it was colored and doctored up, but she said he was argumentative.

About the only time Henry saw the children was on the trips to Chamberstown, and then it was hard to get them to talk about anything except the activities at the new school that had liberated them from the prison of the old one-room school where Henry had gone. That night, as he slipped into bed beside Esther, he reached out in the darkness for her hand and squeezed it. If she responded in any way, Henry told himself, he would open his heart and tell her how lonely and unhappy the good things in life had made him. She never moved and, feeling all alone and very small, Henry turned over and soon fell asleep.

Chapter XII
HENRY COMMUNICATES

As though Henry didn't have enough problems in his life, there was yet another to add to his miseries. The telephone company sent a representative to see him. The power company's progressive move on Salem Pike had prompted them to match the progress in the community and the telephone line was at long last to become a reality. Henry listened without too much enthusiasm—not because he was opposed to progress, but because he wondered how much progress he could stand. He heard the most reasonable arguments as to why he should have a phone installed.

Esther, determined that she would not influence Henry in this, was having a hard time keeping still when she thought of all the added convenience a phone would give them. If there ever were good things in life, a telephone must be one of them. The man from the phone company told them how by telephone they could keep in touch anytime with anyone in the world . . . a real life saver in emergencies. They were told that to be cut off from human contact is to live but a part of life, for the wonder of telephone is that it multiplies human contact (a fact soon to be realized by Henry) and constantly develops new ones. They were told about the wonderful new extensions and that one in the bedroom was a must.

Henry asked why he must be kept constantly in touch with three billion people. Esther laughed, and the phone man winked at her and said times were changing and that progress demanded instant communication. Henry thought of the inability to communicate with his own family and wondered what he should say to three billion people outside his home. Then the telephone man told Henry to think of his wife seriously ill and what a life saver the phone would be to call a doctor to her bedside (this was before Henry had ever tried to call a doctor to *anybody's* bedside). The loud extension bell that could easily be installed at the barn, to keep Henry within earshot of the telephone, seemed also like a good idea and so the contract was signed in Henry's tired signature "Henry L. Morgan" and in Esther's fine little hand "Esther A. Morgan" on the line below.

The next day the phone company installed the phone, and Esther spent the entire day calling everyone she knew on the pike and then started on Willoughby. Henry had never seen her so happy, nor so tired when supper time came, and she confessed that she was so tired she wondered if Henry and the children would mind a few fried eggs for supper. "After all," she explained, "you don't get a telephone every day and have the ability to keep in touch with the whole world." Henry thought to himself that he was real glad this didn't happen every day and hoped it would never happen again.

In the weeks ahead, Henry learned that the same road that let them *out* to Chamberstown, Willoughby and Dexter City soon let all of Chamberstown, Willoughby and Dexter City *in* to them. He also learned that the same little black phone that kept them in touch with the world kept the world in touch with them. More and more time was consumed on the phone. Henry kept an accurate account one rainy day while he was in the house, and the phone rang 17 times. There were solicitors with guessing games and free prizes; TV and radio quiz programs with money to give away; there were calls of inquiry about whether Henry had any lots to sell along the road.

The one call that distressed Henry most was from the assessor's office to inform him that his real estate had been re-appraised in light of the progress that had come to this area; and that instead of the $31 per year, which he and his father had paid for 50 years, his taxes would now amount to $365.78 per year. When Henry protested that it was the same land he had always paid taxes on, they replied, "Not any more it isn't, Henry. You own 160 acres of sub-division land now and that is what progress has done for you." When Henry objected that he had no interest or thought of sub-dividing his farm, they only chuckled and said, "Not now, you don't, but we'll give you time."

Esther had been invited to join the Canasta Club in Willoughby (a game she had never heard of, but was attended by many of her old school friends). She joined and said that everybody needs to get out once in a while by themselves. She also took an active part in the PTA, for they called every Tuesday to see what she could bring on the next home-room mothers' day. She explained she wouldn't have time to bake anything, but she would bring some bakery cookies. This necessitated a trip to Willoughby the next morning.

In the 17 times the phone rang that day, Henry observed that all of them together did not amount to a hill of beans; but that 4 hours and 15 minutes of Esther's life and his had become involved in these nuisance interruptions.

Time was becoming a scarce commodity and more and more he heard himself saying, "I don't have *time.*" Sometimes it seemed like his mind would burst. Like a backlog of trash, the many problems that lay against the dam of his mind threatened to break him and destroy him. If only he could talk it out with Esther, but there was no *time.* No time to think and no time to figure out what had happened at Whispering Pines.

One day, while working in the hayfield, Henry decided that he must talk it out with Esther. He thought how he would come home early from the field and after supper he would suggest that they walk to the point overlooking the valley, and there beneath the big pines he loved so well, he and Esther would tell each other the fears, dreams, hopes and needs of their hearts, just like the old days. The very thought of it made Henry's eyes misty with tears and, like a homesick boy homeward bound, he whistled through the afternoon with a heart light as a feather.

When he arrived home, the children were on the floor before the TV watching as some cowboys thundered through Eagle Pass, and for a while he had a hard time making himself heard. Finally striding over to the TV, he snapped it off and asked, "Where's your mother?" Hilda looked up and said dryly, "Didn't you read the note on the table?" Henry went into the kitchen as the sound of gunshots again echoed throughout the house. Finding a note on the table, he unfolded it to read, in Esther's fine hand, "Dear Henry, Mrs. Snider called from Chamberstown and asked me to help in a special drive for funds for the National Committee for the Mentally Retarded, and I've gone to Chamberstown for the evening. I would have told you, but you were in the hay field and it was so hot, and I didn't have time. There are some TV dinners in the freezer. Hilda knows how to warm them. Don't wait up. I'll be late. Love you, Esther."

Henry's eyes filled with tears and his heart with resentment as he remembered happier days when a walk to the hay field would have been a happy treat for Esther; and he could almost see through his tears her happy figure tripping across the field with a jug of cool water and the greeting, "I just couldn't wait until evening to see you. Let the horses rest and sit in the shade with me for a few minutes." He recalled how they often sat beneath the old oak in the south 40 and reconfirmed their love as the breeze blew through Esther's hair, and how they dreamed and loved and lived.

In a moment he crumpled the note and dashed it into the paper basket by the door. He shouted, "I'm going to the barn to work. I don't want any supper!" He went out and no one heard him slam the door for it sounded just like the gun shots on TV. But Henry didn't go to the barn. He walked in the dark of the evening to the point called Shiloh that overlooked the valley, where the tall pines grew; and there he sat, chewing grass and thinking until the sun went down and the moon came up. The more he thought, the more confused he became and soon he grew weary; and trudging home he slipped into the house and into bed and no one knew he had returned—in fact, no one knew he had been gone.

Chapter XIII

THE COMPLICATIONS OF THE GOOD THINGS

The months sped by—Jeff made the football team the following year, Brent was in Boy Scouts and Hilda in the Campfire Girls. These meetings seemed to keep the whole family going in different directions, for Esther had to do most of the driving. Henry confined himself more and more to his work, for it was a losing battle to keep up with the payments and make ends meet. His gasoline bill was astronomical, and he felt that the slightest financial crisis would all but bankrupt him.

Then it came—not a major catastrophe, but a series of minor things that added up to a major crisis in Henry's life. It all began when he awoke in the middle of the night and, as was his custom since the new plumbing was installed, lay there for a moment to listen to the sounds of the house. The house no longer sounded like the home he had known as a boy, nor like the happy home he had known as a man. The familiar creak of the old house; the squeaking of the porch swing (long since removed) upon its rusty hook; the branches of the big pine scraping across the screen of his bedroom window; the soft, lonesome call of the whippoorwill; and the multitude of night noises that had once acted as a tranquilizer upon the tired mind and body of Henry . . . they were all gone. He couldn't even hear the stately sound of the 80-year-old clock in the living room that had so faithfully told the hour for so many years. In their place was a new sound—the sound of a well-oiled, expensive machine and he had become the chief engineer. No, that was not quite the way it was. Henry thought about it and concluded that he was not *master* of all he heard, but *servant* to it!

While this enlightening thought was yet upon his mind, he heard it—the steady whirr of the pump. He got up, noted that it was 3:00 A.M. and pulled his pants on reluctantly. Picking up a flashlight in the kitchen, he trudged out to the old spring house and opened the door to discover that the pump was running full speed. It was hot and there was no pressure showing on the gauge that told you how much water pressure was being delivered to the marvelous plumbing system in Henry's house. He panicked at the very thought of added expense.

As he made his way out of the spring house, his light fell momentarily upon the jagged end of pipe that had once delivered the free, cool, spring water into the old pitcher pump, now in the junk pile in the old wash over the hill. It was Henry who had sawed it in two as the final act of liberation from the old-fashioned way of life from which he had been delivered into the good things of life. He went back to his bed and, as a tear trickled down his cheek, he wished he had never heard of progress.

The next morning bright and early Esther called him to tell him that the commode wouldn't flush; the lavatory wouldn't provide water for the children to wash; the coffee couldn't be made; and the washer wouldn't work. Henry told her he had discovered it before she had and he would do something about it. He thought of that field that *had* to be mowed today; for rain was due in three days and there was only enough time to get that good hay in the barn before the weather broke. Frustration and then resentment filled his heart as he went to the phone and called the plumber. They were sure they could get to him by Friday; but this was only Tuesday and what did they expect him to do for water in the meantime? They were sure they didn't know. Henry was sure he didn't know either. In desperation, he asked to speak with the man who sold him the plumbing. After some stalling, he came to the phone and Henry once more told him his problem, to which the man indifferently replied, "Look, all of our customers are in desperate circumstances. We'll get to you as soon as we can—O.K.? After all, you're not the only person we sold plumbing to." In anger Henry told Esther she would have to make out the best she could, he had a field to mow and it wouldn't keep. She retorted, "Well, your precious field can wait. I have a washing to do before the Canasta meeting today, a bath to take and —" "Oh, *damn* your Canasta Club and your bath and your everlasting running around and your lousy house!!" Henry found himself shouting to his own surprise. He flew out the door, slamming it behind him and ran to the barn as his eyes filled with tears. It was the first time he could remember ever having raised his voice to Esther. What was wrong with him? Why was he so irritable and short-tempered? Why was he constantly frustrated within and angry with everything and everyone?

Ashamed, he came home late that evening and Esther was especially cool to him, as he expected her to be, and for which he could not blame her. The children were busy with TV; and his supper, what there was of it, was cold. He ate in silence and went to his room to read so that he would not interrupt the children in the living room. They never saw him go upstairs and later Hilda asked, "Did Daddy ever come in?" Jeff said, "Seems like I haven't seen him for weeks. Where does he keep himself?" Henry tried to read but the words blurred before his eyes. He tried to think but thoughts wouldn't come. He turned out the lights, but trying to sleep without Esther was like trying to breathe without air. So he just lay there in the darkness—afraid, confused and not certain about anything or anyone.

While Esther was still in bed the next morning, Henry had a cup of instant coffee by himself and hurried to the barn. The horses had gotten out during the night and had eaten or trampled down most of the small sweet corn patch next to the barn; and so the day didn't start off too well. He harnessed them to the mowing machine, determined that he would get his good hay laid down today—no matter what. Just as he was ready to leave the barn lot, Hilda came running to the barn to tell him that he was wanted on the phone. When he got there, out of breath, he was greeted by a man wanting the Mr. Morgan that sells chickens; and since Henry didn't sell chickens, he was sure he had the wrong number. Henry went slowly back to the barn wondering whose idea it was to put him in instant touch with three billion human beings.

Going to the field, he made great progress. The sky was clear, the breeze warm and the sun bright. The mowing machine clicked beautifully. As he decided to make one more round before lunch, he felt a sudden snap. He stopped to examine the mower and found he had snagged a small stump that he knew was there, but somehow had forgotten in his preoccupation. The stump had done its work, and the drag bar had broken neatly in two, and Henry felt like crying. The field of good hay half down, with bad weather on the way according to the last TV weather bulletin, and a broken mower! Finding a piece of baling wire large enough to hold it together, he started for the barn, trying to work out some emergency plan. There was but one thing to do and that was to get to town as quickly as possible and buy a part for the mower.

He unhitched the horses, put them in the barn and almost ran to the house. When he arrived, the first thing he noticed was that the car was gone. A note on the round kitchen table told him the bad news: "Henry, I've gone to Chamberstown to visit friends. Since you were going to be in the hay field all day, and since you never did anything about the plumbing, I can't stay here without water. There are plenty of TV dinners in the freezer. Will be back when school is out. Esther." This was all he needed. His mind working like clockwork, he tried to think who she might be visiting. Making three calls to the most likely places and getting no results, he sat down on the kitchen chair and stared out into space. With a burst of inspiration, he ran to the phone and called the only tractor dealer in Chamberstown who carried parts for his mower. The man told him that the part wasn't in stock, but that it *was* in stock in Dexter City (27 miles from Chamberstown). The best he could do was to call and have them put it on the evening bus and Henry could pick it up tomorrow. Agreeing reluctantly, he hung up wondering what would happen next . . . he didn't have to wait long to find out.

Going to the freezer, he discovered that the TV dinner he had chosen for his lunch was soft and flabby, which even to Henry didn't seem right. Returning swiftly to the freezer and raising the lid, he saw what he was afraid he would see—*everything* in the freezer was soft and flabby. It was still plugged in; the electricity was still on; and beyond that Henry couldn't know what was wrong. He raced to the phone and dialed the power company only to be told he had the wrong number, that he really wanted to call the *appliance* division. He called the right number and got the wrong people; for this time, he was told he wanted appliance *repair* department. He hung up and dialed the repair department to find the line busy. Five more attempts in the next half hour produced the same results. Finally in desperation he called the operator and asked her to check the line. She did and found out that it was temporarily out of order. Like a cornered animal, Henry decided he wasn't whipped yet. He called the power company and told them his problem, and they agreed to send someone to the repair division with the message. They would get in touch and said for Henry to stay close to the phone. He did and, after eating his soggy TV dinner and drinking two cups of instant coffee, there wasn't much to do but pace the floor and think about the good things in life that had come to him.

He remembered how the old cellar house had never quit running and the cool, free spring water had always flowed into his house without fail, and he wondered if the time and labor-saving devices had really saved him time, labor, money or *anything*. Henry felt angry, frustrated and unhappy. If only Esther were here and he could hear her say, "Don't worry, Henry. Nothing will change as long as we don't change." "Then we *must* be changing," Henry concluded out loud, "for our life has surely changed . . . ." He wondered how it could be when he had been so determined not to change. Henry had never discovered that there was an outside influence at work changing him and Esther—an influence neither one could fight.

His thoughts were interrupted by the demanding ring of the phone, and Henry answered to hear an efficient man from the power company on the other end—"Did you call for the repair division, Mr. Morgan?" Henry said he surely had, and that his deep freeze was not working . . . no, he didn't know how long it had not been working . . . yes, he had looked at the plug . . . no, he had not checked the fuse because everything else was working . . . yes, he was sure the electricity was on because he had just warmed water for instant coffee. The man said it was now past three o'clock and there would be no chance of coming today, but he would get to him sometime tomorrow. When Henry pressed him to come sooner, explaining that he had a whole beef plus many other food items in that freezer, the man sympathetically told him that there was a widow with seven children on Laurel Fork whose deep freeze had been out for three days and they were *still* trying to get to her. But, he assured Henry, though they were snowed under, they were doing the best they could—what with two men on vacation and all . . . . Henry silently wished he were literally snowed under and then the freezer would be no problem. Since there was nothing more to say, Henry said to come as soon as possible, and the man said by noon tomorrow at the latest.

While Henry was unharnessing the horses at the barn, Esther came in driving very slowly and he met her just as she was getting some things out of the back seat. "Oh, hi, Henry," she said. "Would you mind helping me out with these things?" He said he would help and filled his arms with things and wanted to ask what they were, but thought he didn't dare. She put his mind at ease. "Lois and I went to Seers to look around this afternoon, and you know those curtains I have been wanting for the living room? Well, they were on sale. They weren't the color I wanted but they'll do. And, Henry, wait 'til you see the darling dresses for Hilda that were on sale too!" Henry thought she had plenty of dresses; and Esther reminded him that she was hard to fit, and she had to buy them when she could find them. Henry also wondered why the new sewing machine was in the stair closet all packed away, but then Esther *was* plenty busy most of the time. He carried the things into the house; and as he started out again, Esther dropped the bomb—"Henry, I want to tell you. There's something funny wrong with the car. I thought it wasn't going to start when I came out of Seers. It just made a funny groaning noise, and I noticed that all day the little red light has been on." He said he would see about it and he did. The battery was dead; and so he went in and, after a phone call to the garage in Willoughby, he discovered that the generator was probably not operating. Henry did not know too much about generators; but, after a little information from the garage man, Henry got his tools and tried to take it off. It was a hard job with only a pipe wrench and some open-end wrenches; but, after only two busted knuckles, Henry got it off. Even he could smell the burnt wiring and knew he had found the trouble.

He called the man at the garage, but in the meantime it had closed; though Henry did succeed in getting Fred Danner on the line, and Fred said he could ride to town tomorrow morning with him if he wanted to take the generator. Henry said he would have to whether he wanted to or not, for he had to get to Chamberstown tomorrow for the part for the mower.

Agreeing on 8:30 in the morning, Henry sat down to his cold supper alone. After supper, he drifted into the living room and took a seat in the corner. He hoped that maybe they could talk a little on the porch, like they used to, but then the porch wasn't too good a place to sit. The noise of the traffic was bad for one thing and then Esther said she didn't like to sit out there where everyone could stare at you when they went by; and, furthermore, if you sat out there very long, somebody would take it as an invitation to visit the rest of the evening, and nobody felt up to that.

He noticed that the program they were watching was just about over and he was determined that he would suggest a "family night" as soon as the commercial started. In a few minutes he blurted out, "Anybody for dominoes?"—no answer. "How about a good checker game?" The children began to say to each other, "Why don't you play Daddy a game?" and were answering with "Why don't *you?*" Finally, Esther said in an apologetic voice, "I think they were wanting to watch 'The Virginian,' Henry." "Boy, Dad, you will really love it," said Jeff. "It's about the outdoors." Henry decided that maybe he really would enjoy it, so he settled back in his chair, but during the first gun battle he fell asleep.

Esther roused him to tell him the eleven o'clock news was just coming on and he had better get to bed, if he was going to go with Fred Danner the next day. As he sat on the edge of the bed he said, without turning around, "Esther, I'm sorry about yesterday and the things I said. I don't know why I lost my temper, but I've been so nervous and irritable lately. I can't sleep like I used to, and there have been so many things on my mind." She sat down and put her arms around him and said, "I understand, Henry. Part of it was my fault, and I'm sorry too. I love you, and I want you to feel like your old self again. I've noticed that you've been tired and run down lately and, while I was in town, I stopped to see Dr. Manson. He said you should come in for a check-up right away, and I promised him I would speak to you about it."

Now, Henry couldn't remember when he had ever been to a doctor. He had his tonsils out when he was a boy and that seemed to be the only time he could recall; but he was past 40 now, and a man's health *does* change. With Esther's concern so obvious, Henry soon agreed to see Dr. Manson for that check-up; and, kissing Esther good night, he was soon asleep.

Chapter XIV

THE PLOT THICKENS

Events moved swiftly the next few days and weeks. The car cost Henry two days' involvement plus $48; and the well had caved in, the man said (who finally came after they had been out of water for six days) and that was very costly—to be exact, around $480. The electric man said that the unit had gone bad in the freezer and that this often happened even in new ones, for no matter how well things are built there is always a lemon, he reminded Henry. Of course the freezer was under warranty and there was only a $25 service call, but unfortunately the food was not under warranty and so Henry lost the beef which had all thawed out. Since the weather was around 90 degrees at the time, it didn't take it long to go bad. Henry argued that the power company should be responsible, but they said Henry should have called as soon as the freezer went out and Henry said he didn't know about it and they said they couldn't help that and so he gave up and gave in.

By the time he had repaired his mowing machine and finished the field, the bad weather had come, and it rained seven days running on the good hay he had counted on for the cattle next winter. By the time the rain had stopped, the hay was black and beaten into the ground so badly that Henry raked it and burned it in the windrow. That was the day he sat down in the barn where no one could see him or hear him and sobbed with his face in his hands. It was not the sobbing of sorrow as much as it was of frustration and a loneliness that he couldn't explain. He tried to explain to Dr. Manson how he felt and couldn't. Dr. Manson was sympathetic, and said Henry was working too hard and was nervous, and so he prescribed some tranquilizers for Henry and some little white pills that would "help him get a good night's sleep", but he was not to take them unless he was desperate for sleep. Henry found himself more desperate as the days went by. His appetite seemed to be growing worse, and he noticed that when he ate certain foods his stomach burned and pained and he had constant headaches. One thing helped though—he learned from TV all the popular remedies, and his medicine cabinet soon boasted a small, well-stocked pharmacy. There were three or four kinds of headache medicines for his three or four kinds of headaches, his tranquilizers, sleeping tablets, anti-acid medicines for the stomach distress he had so frequently, laxatives and, of course, the latest in cold medicines.

The next crisis came when he sat down and realistically looked at his financial situation. He had never really done this and somehow the "buy now—pay later plan" and its full significance had never really grasped Henry. At the round table, late at night, he was shocked by the actual figures. The bills that had been coming had been hurriedly stuffed in what Henry had termed his "bill box." (In reality it was the neat little box in which he brought Esther candy from Wigal's General Store on Valentine's Day a long time ago.) When he poured the bills out on the table along with the payment books and duplicate credit cards that had accumulated in the months past, Henry saw a formidable mountain built out of the small stones of miscellaneous bills. A quick tally told him the story; approximately $285 per month in regular obligations and an accumulation of nearly $1,000 in miscellaneous bills including the large one for the well. The book from the bank lay in front of him as a mute reminder of a $7500 mortgage he saw no possible way of ever paying, not even in the 20 allotted years.

Trying not to panic, Henry thought, "There *has* to be a way out and I've *got* to find it!!" Esther came in from the PTA meeting and said, "What are you into?" Henry said, "Just looking at our obligations and frankly, Esther, I'm scared to death." "Scared of what, Henry? It's not as bad as you imagine. Everything's all right. Remember, Henry, we have each other; and as long as *we* don't change nothing will change. We have Whispering Pines, the children and all the good things in life and these bills are just one of the costs involved in it all. Think how thankful we should be that the Lord made all these good things possible for us. Remember how it was before?" With a sickness creeping over his heart that he couldn't explain, Henry *did* remember. He closed his eyes, and he could see himself walking behind the mares on a spring day . . . the sun shining, the earth bursting forth in its clean green suit of life; the happy waters of Sycamore Creek bubbling with pent-up enthusiasm; birds singing their chorus; and most of all, TIME . . . TIME to hear and see it all and to take it all in. He remembered the unhurried evenings on the porch; the plaintive note of the whippoorwill; the night with its soothing noises like a tranquilizer upon his heart. He remembered how it used to be when the children were tucked in and he and Esther sat on the porch and talked . . . loved and lived. He remembered how, with mind and heart clear, he lay down with the smell of honeysuckle drifting through the open window and slept . . . and slept. Henry wished he could just once more capture that time and that he could be in his bed like he used to be and morning would never come.

With a return to reality Henry suddenly realized that he was not remembering "how it was before" like Esther was; and he didn't know how to tell her what "progress" had done for him, or rather *to* him.

He explained to Esther that their monthly obligations far exceeded their income and that there was no possible way to balance such a swollen budget. They talked and figured and schemed, and came to the conclusion that Henry *must* have more income if they were to make ends meet. He was yet to learn that whenever he found out how to make ends meet, something would move the middle again. The needed income could be realized, if Henry could speed up production on the farm. He said *time* was what he needed desperately. He said he couldn't understand where the time went. No sooner did he get in the field, until it was evening. The deep involvement of the "things" he possessed had done its work in whittling Henry's day from 12 full, free, wonderful hours, to a few jammed with troubles and problems. Each day he slipped farther and farther behind. The fields were running down, the cattle were only half cared for and the fences almost all needed replacing. Finally, they reluctantly agreed that the mares were costing Henry lots of valuable time. By the time he caught them in the morning, brushed them, talked to them, fed them, harnessed them and was ready to go to the field, an hour and a half had been wasted. Henry had never thought of this time as "wasted" before . . . especially since Old Brown had been killed. He looked forward to the time; for the horses remained in his mind as one of the few things that had not changed. Always the same, they linked him to happier times. He talked to them often, as he would have talked to Esther if she had the time; but the mares were never in a hurry. Somehow they had remained stable and strong, and he was sure that nothing would ever change them. But, facts are stubborn things . . . they don't change. The fact was that they had served their usefulness, and a tractor was the only answer to speeding up a slowed production. With the decision made, they planned how to accomplish this; and the only answer seemed to be a second mortgage on Whispering Pines. Henry agreed to see Will Jenkins first thing in the morning.

The morning came, as it always does, and it was raining. This relieved Henry somewhat of the guilt of spending another day of involvement instead of doing the many things that needed done. On the way to Chamberstown he thought of the help he needed and wished the boys would show more interest in the farm. He couldn't blame them too much. There was so much to do. The football and basketball schedules were time-consuming, and Esther was right in saying that they only go to school once and shouldn't be saddled down with responsibility. Hilda helped some around the house, but it was the farm that worried Henry. He had heard the boys talking one night while he was in the kitchen and they were in the dining room working on their homework. Brent had said he didn't understand why Henry wanted to mess around with that old worn-out farm, when other men were working only 40 hours a week at the plant in Chamberstown and making five times as much money. Jeff had agreed, and said he sure never wanted to be stuck in the country for life, and that he was going to college and make something of himself. These things had hurt Henry; but he was being hurt so much lately that he wondered if he was overly sensitive. He remembered what Dr. Manson had told him and he figured his nervous condition accounted for most of it. After all, the boys would have to decide what's best for themselves. As for himself, he had made his decision years ago while trailing along behind his father in the south 40 as he plowed one spring. He would never leave Whispering Pines, and Shiloh would be his final resting place.

Soon he was talking with Will Jenkins and reluctantly Will agreed to an additional loan of $3,000. Henry explained that $1,000 would be used to pay off an accumulation of bills and $2,000 for a proposed tractor and equipment. With the sale of his grey mares he hoped to have a little to go on and "tide him over," as his dad used to say. Will talked frankly about the easy credit system and what it was doing to people; but Henry said he didn't intend for it to ever change him, and this situation in his life was only temporary. Soon, with the new tractor and all, things would change, he was sure. And they did.

The new mortgage was for 5 years at 7% and all in all totaled $4,050 at 60 payments of $67.50. This increased Henry's obligation to around $352 per month, but he was sure he would overcome the increase as well as meet the standing obligation with a new tractor. Well, not really new, for new ones cost twice the amount Henry had to spend. He was fortunate to find a tractor with the necessary implements in fair shape for the $2,000 he had to spend. It was ten years old, but the man said models didn't make any difference to a tractor; and Henry could see that it didn't as long as the tractor worked good. And this tractor did. It kind of scared Henry at first . . . so much power at his finger tips and he had to go slow until he "got the feel of it." The boys showed their first interest in the farm for a long time, for they were fascinated with that tractor. They wanted to help as long as they could try their hand at the tractor, which Henry didn't allow too much; for it was the only means he had of making out. They never understood this and often murmured to Esther that, "Dad sure is tight with that old tractor."

Henry had his disappointment too. When he hired Bill Baxter to take the mares to the sale for him, he was shocked to see that they only brought $75 apiece. Henry was so angry he almost cried in public when the hammer fell and those strong, honest, good mares went for such a pittance. When he loudly complained to the men around him, he was quickly told that nobody wants a pair of old work mares. "What good are they?" they said, "Nobody needs them any more." Henry came home and never told anyone that when he went to the barn to put the tractor away, he couldn't bring himself to talk to it. He went into the big, empty box stall that had belonged for so many years to those wonderful grey mares and cried. Nor did he ever tell them that each time he went to the barn to get the tractor, he had to turn his head so he couldn't see the harness, now covered with cobwebs and chaff, hanging in the stall. Somehow one of the last links with Whispering Pines as it used to be was broken forever.

Chapter XV

THE PRESSURE MOUNTS

Henry threw himself into the farm with resolve to get on top of those bills and to make Whispering Pines the most productive farm in Mindoah County. This wouldn't have been too hard for not many folk farmed any more. The more attractive offers of employment in a now bustling, booming Chamberstown had drawn from the farms most of the able-bodied men. "Why work from daylight till dark for mere food, clothing and shelter, when we can work forty hours a week and have all the good things in life and time to enjoy them," was their argument. Somehow it had not worked that way yet with Henry, but he hoped it would soon.

More disappointment was yet to come . . . like the day the tractor broke down and he learned it had thrown a rod, whatever that was. The $289 repair bill would just have to be worked out on payments, the garage man said. He couldn't face the prospects of seeing Will Jenkins at the bank; so the good garage man introduced him to Easy Finance, the nice people with money. After talking to the manager, Henry learned that the interest rates were higher, but the convenience of only a signature attracted him. So, pressed by the need of the tractor, he just couldn't resist. The $391 note for 24 months came to only $16 per month and Henry felt he could absorb this.

The money from the mares soon ran out; and, with other purchases following logically in place, Henry was soon swamped. It all seemed so easy. For instance, he found that he couldn't keep up with the yard in the summertime, and Esther seemed to think it was too much for the boys. Anyway they went to Little League and swimming classes at the new pool in Chamberstown, and when they were home they had to have time to play. So Henry bought a new power mower at Seers; and Esther got wall-to-wall carpet for the house, because the Canasta Club had elected her president and planned to meet once every two weeks at Whispering Pines. Esther hadn't really asked for the carpet; but when she spoke of the shabby floors and the hand-woven throw rugs Henry's mother had made, and of the new home one of the girls lived in at Willoughby, Henry got the message. He surely didn't want to deprive anyone of the good things in life, and he didn't want his family taking a back seat to anyone. So the carpet became a reality, and it necessitated a vacuum cleaner and the permanent removal of Henry's gum boots. One thing led to another, and Henry began to sell off the white-face cattle one by one; now his present herd was down to seven and still he couldn't make it. Added to all of this was the fact that Henry's car was going day and night and the tires had been replaced, and how it looked like soon the whole car would have to be replaced. Someone suggested they do like the Danners had done and buy a second car so it would not be so hard on the one. They even suggested one of those "little foreign cars" that didn't use too much gas. It sounded pretty good, and Henry thought about it; but he couldn't catch Esther long enough to talk it over with her.

Another thing was bothering Henry. It seemed like home had become a madhouse of activity. The plagued phone rang incessantly, and every phone call brought another realm of involvement with one of the three billion human beings out there in the outside world. The house ran to extremes. It was either frantic, frustrating activity—or somber, tomb-like silence that made Henry lonesome. The world of modern conveniences brought deeper and deeper involvement in *time* and *thought*, and the car brought continued involvement in a growing geographical circle. It seemed to Henry, as he squatted by Sycamore Creek one afternoon all alone, that his life was like the stone he tossed into the clear waters. The ripples reached out further and further and lapped against the shores, and the stone was swallowed forever. He felt like he had been thrown into a stream of life, whose ripples of involvement went out further and further, until they met the shores; and *he* would be swallowed forever. He kept saying to himself that he must keep that from happening.

The big trouble really began to come when Henry came to the house to answer the phone and was reminded by the friendly man at Easy Finance that his payment was past due. Henry explained about the weather and the cattle market, but the now not-so-friendly man didn't know anything about that, or care; all he knew was that the 15th of the month was past by three weeks and Henry's check had not arrived. The man only wanted one word from Henry: "When can we expect your payment?" He also acidly reminded Henry that there was a deed of trust against the tractor, a thing Henry didn't understand, for he had never read the many papers to which he had written, "Henry L. Morgan" and underneath which Esther in her fine hand had written, "Esther A. Morgan."

Will Jenkins sent him a little note that was gentle but firm, and reminded Henry that the payments on both the mortgages were past due; and that in order to keep his account up to date, would he please stop in the bank at his earliest convenience. Henry did. Will explained that he wasn't pressing Henry, but the auditors insisted that the notes be brought up to date. Henry felt like maybe Will could understand; so he poured out the whole story of how the harder he tried, the more involved he became; and the more time and labor-saving devices he acquired, the less time and more labor he seemed to have. He told Will how he had discovered that night in bed that he was not master of all he possessed, but his possessions mastered him, and that he was a slave to the freedom they promised. Will nodded sympathetically and suggested a way for Henry to make out. "Why don't you go to Chamberstown and see if you can get on at General Electronics?" he asked. When the indignation flushed on Henry's face, Will calmed him with this thought: "It need only be for a little while . . . say six months. That's not forever, Henry, then you can go back to Whispering Pines. For the sake of your family and for the good name of your father and yours, Henry, think it over. If you decide you want to do it, I have a little influence in the personnel office, and I'd be glad to see what I can do for you." Then Will took Henry's hand and said, "Henry, your father was a good man and an honest one. You're an honest man too, and I don't want to see you changed or get in any deeper. Think about it."

Henry did think about it all the way home. In fact, he turned in the driveway and never remembered any of the trip from Chamberstown. He didn't see Esther until she came to bed late that night from the planning meeting where she had worked on a new bond issue for the schools. When she came to bed, she was surprised to find Henry still awake. When he told her what Will had said, she lay quiet for a long while. "What do you think I should do, Esther?" he anxiously asked. "I think you should do whatever you feel is best for all of us, Henry. You're the head of the house, and whatever you say is all right with me. We have each other and whatever comes we'll face it together. If you want to do it, I'm with you all the way. I heard some of the girls at the Canasta Club talking about their husbands working there and what good money they were making. It seems like it would be a good change for you, Henry. Instead of fighting that old ground and equipment all day and then not being able to make a living, you could work 40 hours a week and be home to rest and be with the family again. Oh, Henry, I *do* think it's a good idea. Maybe it will bring back the old days. We'll walk to Shiloh in the morning and talk about it." Henry thanked her for standing by him and dropped into an anxious and troubled sleep. He seemed to be having a nightmare in which he found himself standing on an endless, open plain alone. He was free and unrestrained, and he could feel the fresh clear air; suddenly an unseen, undefinable force came from the horizon like a mighty storm, and with a terrible sound, increasing as it approached, it came closer, closer . . . and closer until, at the exact moment it was ready to consume Henry totally, he awoke. The sweat poured down his face and, with eyes wide with fear, he groped for Esther's hand in the darkness. It was there, but she was asleep. Next morning he tried to tell her about it, but the bus was coming and the children had to catch it. After they left he wanted to tell her, but the phone rang. It was Lois Kimball, and they planned a shopping trip. Esther promised to hear about Henry's dream that night; and so the morning walk to Shiloh was forgotten.

Chapter XVI

HENRY FINDS THE ANSWER

Henry went to Chamberstown and to General Electronics after stopping by the bank to tell Will of his plans. Will was delighted, and by the time Henry arrived at the personnel office, he felt like a special person. The secretary said, "Are you Henry Morgan?" to which he replied he was; then she said sweetly, "Come right in—Mr. Perkins is expecting you." Henry went in and was met by a friendly man who seemed to reek of self-confidence and enthusiasm. He gripped Henry's hand and ushered him to a nice overstuffed chair. The man said Will Jenkins had called from the bank and had given Henry a high recommendation. They chatted awhile, and then he asked Henry what kind of work he was qualified to do. Henry couldn't think of any and told him he had never known anything but outside work on the farm, and asked if he had any outside work. Mr. Perkins said not really, but that the inside work was pleasant enough, and Henry would get used to it. Soon Mr. Perkins had Henry take some tests and three hours later forms were filled out, and he was asked to sign in triplicate the forms of employment on the desk, which he did. With a hand that was unsure, he wrote "Henry L. Morgan," and noticed there was no line underneath for Esther to sign, and he felt that this was his to do alone this time. He knew she agreed with him; but oh, how he wished she was sitting there and would soothe his troubled heart and the fear that gnawed away in the pit of his stomach. Mr. Perkins said there were some other matters to attend to and that he should come back next day for a physical, income tax forms, social security matters, health insurance, work clothes, safety shoes and shots. It seemed like so many unnecessary details to just do a day's work for a company, but Mr. Perkins assured him that all employees had to do the same.

Henry came back the next day, and by noon he was ready to go to work with a shiny new identification badge with his picture and his own special number "97577." After that, he learned everything in the plant would be geared to that number. He saw Mr. Perkins go through the plant that afternoon and Henry spoke to him; but he must have been preoccupied because he acted like he couldn't remember Henry, or didn't want to. The plant doctor called Henry in that afternoon and told him that he was afraid he had ulcers and was badly run down and needed vitamins. These he could obtain at a reduced rate for employees. So, armed with all he needed, he went home to tell Esther all about the strange world of industry to which he had been introduced. At least he *wanted* to tell her, but she was in Willoughby for the Canasta Club meeting and had left a TV dinner to thaw for him. The children were at Danners for the evening and the old house was empty . . . silent, except for the steady hum of the many time and labor-saving machines and devices that filled the house. Henry thought of them and his heart sank as he remembered how clear it was that *they* had mastered *him*.

The first day on the job was a disappointment to Henry. He had hoped he would get a job more to his liking, but he didn't. They put him in a room with 100 other employees all doing the same job. Henry's job was to stand at a drill press, take little black objects of bakelite from a conveyor belt in front of him and drill a hole in each corner of them. Of course he had to do it at such a speed to keep up with the speed of the belt moving endlessly before him. It bothered him at first, for it reminded him too much of his own life. The pressure of that endless belt carrying its constant responsibilities . . . the pressure upon him to keep up with it all and never getting anywhere really; for the more he drilled, the more un-drilled objects came at him. For awhile in the afternoon he panicked and thought about fleeing to Whispering Pines and Shiloh to think about whether he really wanted this job or not. Terrible claustrophobia crept over him and sweat broke out in the palms of his hands. He signaled to the foreman, explaining that he didn't feel well. He asked if he could take a few minutes rest. The foreman told Henry that he understood and most new employees usually had some trouble adjusting. He explained that the dust from the bakelite Henry was drilling sometimes created a stuffy feeling; but he assured Henry that sooner or later he would get used to it—"So much so," he said, "you will never hear the noise around you or smell the bakelite dust." Henry prayed under his breath that God would forbid him ever coming to such a place in his life.

Since Henry had made the break with the "old life," he was sure that things would be different and that the constant involvements would not bother him, now that he was on a schedule. *Schedule* was right, for he was working shift work, a thing altogether new to Henry and kind of weird at first. It was strange coming home at midnight while on the 3 to 11 shift, warming some hot dogs, opening a can of soup, drinking a Coke and eating alone in a quiet house. Or, stranger yet was the night shift, coming home in the morning with the sun shining brightly and the out-of-doors beckoning, and closing the blinds in a hot bedroom and trying to sleep. This was one thing Henry couldn't get used to, so he stayed up a lot on the night shift, and his weight began to drop due to the loss of sleep. His eyes showed it too. He took more and more of the tranquilizers, and when desperate (a word Dr. Manson first used), more of the little white pills that helped him to get a good night's sleep. Sometimes when he woke up after such a night, he felt like he was groggy and dizzy and noticed his reactions were slower than usual. Of course, Henry reasoned, he was getting older. He was pushing 50 pretty hard and that's bound to tell on a man.

As time went on the involvements became more critical than ever before. There were union dues and monthly meetings, and then there was the lodge. Henry had lived all his life without the lodge and didn't really understand what it was all about. He was in the lunchroom one day when the foreman asked him if he had ever thought about joining. Henry said he had thought about a lot of things in his time but that wasn't one of them. The lodge was explained in such a way that it left Henry with a distinct impression that to belong would give him an edge over others in the society he found himself in. He felt the message was that it would even help him to advance on his job. Advance was something he needed, for the six months he intended to stay on the job already stretched into two years, and the longer he worked the harder it was to make any headway toward his heart's desire: to return to Whispering Pines and Shiloh's peace.

Henry was forced to buy a second car, and about the time he got to where he could handle it the family insisted on color TV. They reminded him that it was certainly no fun to sit home every evening, while he worked shift work, and not be able to see TV in *color*. Many of the time and labor-saving devices he had first purchased had to be replaced, and it was constantly one thing after another. In desperation he sold the tractor, consolidated all his obligations with a regular bank loan and settled his mind to another two years at General Electronics before his long-dreamed-of return to Whispering Pines. So, when the foreman told him about the lodge and the opportunity it afforded to "get ahead," Henry decided to join. Join he did, and waded through all the childish and meaningless rituals that made him a full-fledged member of the order. He wore his "ring" with hope and he seemed to enjoy some improvement; for soon he was being asked to work overtime, a thing he was never asked to do before. The double shifts were especially hard on him. He coughed a lot, and the plant doctor said the bakelite dust had the same effect on all the employees, but it was nothing to be concerned about. Henry wasn't too much concerned about it either, until one night he took a coughing spell that he could not stop and little flecks of blood appeared on his handkerchief. He never mentioned this to Esther for he saw no need to concern her. She had *so* much to do.

Esther had thrown herself into community affairs for real. She was president of the PTA, served on several advisory committees, active in the Farm Women's Club (a thing Henry never understood for few of the women lived on a farm), helped in all the charity drives and had taken a big part in the enlarged M. E. Church program on Salem Pike. Presently they were trying to build a new Sunday School addition, and she had gladly and proudly obligated Henry for $500 the night they had the pledge banquet. Henry had worked a double that night; but Esther told him, when he came home, how proud she was to be able to speak up and tell the church Henry would have made the pledge had he been there. The minister and some of the trustees came to her and told her to be sure and tell "good old Henry" how much they appreciated it. Henry was pleased and hoped overtime would hold out long enough for him to make his promise good.

It seemed Henry and Esther saw little of each other in the months that followed. She had her life and schedule, and he had his. Like ships passing in the night, the little notes exchanged on the kitchen table often became the only communication they shared for weeks at a time. Once Henry had been so lonely that he went to the phone in the lunchroom and called to just hear her voice and to say he loved her. When she answered and told him to hurry (Lois had just driven up to take her to Willoughby for some shopping), somehow he forgot what he was going to say . . . so he mumbled a few words and hung up.

Sometimes weeks went by without Henry really talking to the children. When he was not in bed or at work, they were gone, or watching the TV or some other involvement. Henry found himself too tired to worry about much of anything any more. Each day at the plant he would promise himself that he would sit down with Esther and beg her help to work out some way to return to Whispering Pines as it used to be. Like a man lost in an impenetrable jungle seeking desperately for direction, he needed help and understanding. Each night when he came home with that determination, something happened to prevent it. A few times he drove straight in the driveway, left his lunch bucket on the seat and walked alone to Shiloh. There, with the valley in all its beauty spreading before him and the fresh air filling his lungs, he sat under the great pines and listened for their sighing. They sighed, and it soothed him; so much so that he fell asleep one night. It was late when he awakened and hurried down to the darkened house, only to fall into bed for the rest he needed to work a double shift the next day.

One day the foreman asked if Henry would like to take a little vacation. He had worked through all his vacation time for four straight years; and the foreman felt, for health reasons, Henry should take some time off. Henry hadn't really thought about it much. His idea was to work until he could take a permanent vacation at Whispering Pines and Shiloh . . . to return to the life he loved and desperately needed. Esther was delighted though and said, "Oh,

Henry, it really will be like old times again . . . you and me and the children together. We can go away and sit down and talk, and you can rest." It sounded like a dream come true, and Henry found out from some of the men at work about the nice camping trailers he could rent for a week or two, and about the camping facilities at the state parks.

After investing in all the usual camping gear, and after excitedly planning for weeks, they were at last off for a two-week vacation that Henry said would be to "get away from it all." Jeff couldn't go of course, for he had a part-time job at the service station to pay for his sports car Henry helped him buy. He spent most of his time in town anyway, but Brent and Hilda were there, and his beloved Esther. With the little trailer behind the new car they had bought that month, they drove happily toward Big Bend State Park, so named for the big bend the river took at that point. Setting their camper on the lot next to the people from another state who had brought a tent, Henry decided he didn't like the close proximity. He soon discovered that the lots were small, and in reality, they were camped on each other's doorstep; but Esther said it was only for a few days, and it was soon forgotten as they adapted themselves to busy camp life. Henry seemed to really enjoy himself. Esther said he looked like a new man when he came up from the river holding three small fish he had caught. Brent reminded him that he could catch bigger ones than that any day of the week back in Sycamore Creek, and Henry's joy faded as the words stung him in his heart. One phrase he kept saying all the time was, "This is really living . . . away from it all." But alas, a man can't find any way to "stay away from it all" forever, and the day soon came when they had to pack up and return home. Henry had spent most of his evenings by the campfire dreaming of Whispering Pines and Shiloh, for the only vacation he ever really wanted was to be back home once more and left alone by the society around him.

After the trip was over and the routine of Henry's life began again, the new-found strength soon ebbed and the luster was again gone from his eyes. He seemed more withdrawn and indifferent to all around him, and he became uncommunicative with others. Esther seemed to feel it was because when he came home he looked into the "bill box" too often, and spent one whole evening trying to figure out how long it would be before he could come back to the farm to stay.

Chapter XVII

HENRY GOES HOME TO SHILOH

I guess the story of Henry and the great society could go on indefinitely, but I feel that I must tell you what happened. I thought at first I wouldn't; but it's only fair that the reader know for himself the end of the whole matter.

One day, as Henry stood at the drill press drilling holes in the little black bakelite boxes, he began to cough and, after calling for relief, went back to the infirmary to lie down for a few minutes. He had been doing this a lot recently and was always tired. While he lay there with his eyes closed, he could hear the continual hum of the plant, and it suddenly reminded him of the hum of his house and how he had discovered that night that he was a slave to an inhuman machine that would destroy him eventually. Now the hum of the plant confirmed what he already knew and would not admit: *he was hopelessly trapped!* Living in a silent world of desperation, Henry knew now that he would *never* go back to Whispering Pines. The unchecked panic of a caged animal seized him, and he turned his face to the wall and openly and unashamedly wept and sobbed. Oh, if Esther could only know. If he could only tell her . . . or somebody. But no one was listening. How could they? The hum of society around him drowned out every plea for help. Esther could not know, for the gap was too great between them. For her the new world of convenience had indeed been good in some ways, and for the children it was a fairyland of excitement. For Henry, though, it was a dreary, desolate prison to which he was forever consigned. He somehow knew how the goose that laid the golden egg must have felt. He saw himself as only a means to the end of the life they enjoyed. He felt crushed . . . lonely, unloved, and above all, misunderstood. Suddenly he saw himself engaged in a life-and-death struggle with the great, affluent society around him. It was the intangible, undefinable, invisible power that sought to destroy him in his nightmare so long ago; and the hot tears streaming down his face told him how close that destruction was.

The infirmary nurse looked in on him and asked, "Mr. Morgan, are you all right?" Henry meekly answered, "Would it matter if I wasn't?" "Why of course it would," replied the nurse. "You're important to us here, Mr. Morgan. The department couldn't make it without you." And somehow, she had told the story of Henry's life. She gave him a shot to help him rest, and when he awakened it was dark. Henry was groggy from the shot, but he told the nurse he thought he could make it. She wanted to call Esther to come for him, but he told her not to bother anyone—that he'd make it alone. He stopped by the lunchroom for a drink of water and took two of the tranquilizers Dr. Manson had given him to "quiet his nerves," and headed for the parking lot. As he was about to get into his car, he looked up (something he had not done for a long time); the moon was full and bright, and the stars were spattered across the sky. He stood there for a moment thinking of that moon and how it would look from Shiloh, flickering its silver beams off the corn shocks in his field. While he stood there looking at the moon, it seemed he could hear the children laughing again, and he could smell the open fire and the freshly popped corn, and he could hear Esther say, "Come, Henry, let's take a moonlight stroll in the cornfield and you can tell the children a story before bedtime." And then it seemed like Esther was in his arms and they were together again, laughing, loving and living. Henry got in his car, longing for the deep rest he had known in those days and for Shiloh. As the engine of his new car came to life, he flicked on his headlights and roared off into the night. Henry was on his way home at last, to Whispering Pines and Shiloh.

Fred Danner said he heard the crash about 10:00 P.M. and thought it was an explosion. Later he thought it might have been a wreck, so he pulled on his pants and grabbed his jacket and flashlight and stepped out into the clear, crisp night. The moon was full and bright, and he did not see or hear anything that alarmed him until his dog began to bark at the bridge that crossed the deepest part of Sycamore Creek. Running to see what it could be, he saw the twisted guard rail and broken glass. When he looked down into the moonlit waters of Sycamore Creek, he saw Henry's car, upside down, its wheels still spinning. Fred listened for some sound of life, but the only sound that broke the stillness of the night was the plaintive call of a whippoorwill and the steady hum of those wheels. Fred later told and retold how he went to the car, but it was too late. Henry was dead and had a peaceful smile that Fred said he hadn't remembered seeing on Henry's face for a long time. The sheriff came, of course, and he was puzzled as to why there were no skid marks found on the pavement to indicate an effort to stop, and how the accelerator was not stuck, but the speedometer was . . . at 60 miles per hour. No signs of mechanical failure were discovered on the car. He finally said he guessed it was an accident. When the nurse told her story of how groggy Henry was when he left the infirmary, and the lunch room waitress told how she had given him a glass of water as he left the plant, and she saw him take two capsules of some kind, and Dr. Manson told the sheriff what they were; everybody seemed sure that they knew the full story.

Esther was on the phone arranging some last-minute details for the cancer fund drive. She was terribly upset over the way cancer was destroying innocent people and no one seemed to care. She heard the noise too, but thought it was a sonic boom. The children didn't hear it at all because they were watching the late movie that was about a psychopathic killer on the loose and how all of society sought to destroy him. Since there was a lot of shooting, the crash was never noticed. Of course Esther went to pieces when she heard what happened, and Dr. Manson had to put her on the same green and white tranquilizers that Henry had been on. He gave her some of the little white pills to help her "get a good night's sleep." Some of the neighbors came, but most of them called on the phone to express their sympathy. The union sent appropriate flowers, and the lodge brothers all called at the funeral home in Chamberstown and had a little ritual. The plant sent a huge bouquet of flowers with a note saying Henry would be sadly missed in Production #2. The funeral director said he had never remembered so many flowers sent for one man with such kind words of sympathy.

Everyone was so kind; and when the day of the funeral arrived, they loaded Henry into a new Cadillac hearse, banked his coffin with flowers and brought him to Salem Pike M. E. Church. The church choir sang and the minister told everyone that Henry was born and raised there, and how he was a good husband and father and had given his family "all the good things in life." He told them how he could remember coming there 20 years ago when Henry didn't have a thing, not even electricity or a car. Then he told some things about Henry's life, how he used to drive an old pair of grey mares, and that he had sure come a long way. He ended by saying what a tragedy his untimely death was, for, he concluded, Henry had everything to live for. He also told how Henry's desire was to be buried at Shiloh, and a grave had been prepared there for him. As it turned out they had quite a time getting up to Shiloh for the burial. They searched far and near but could not find a team of horses to pull a sled to the top of the hill. At last, they found a man with a small dozer to pull the sled up the hill for the funeral director; and Henry was, as many said, finally at rest at his beloved Shiloh.

There was a lot of talk among the people after the funeral. Some still wondered how the "accident" happened, and others said no one would ever know whether it was an accident or not. Fred Danner recounted his story to an eager audience in the church yard and said it sure was ironic that Henry was so close home when it happened. "So close," Fred pressed upon them, "that if he could have looked through that shattered windshield he could have seen the fodder in the shock in his own corn field. That's getting pretty close to home, not to make it," Fred mournfully concluded. My observation is that Henry was farther from home than anyone will ever know; for distance is no longer measured in this society by miles.

There's one more thing you should know. After the funeral was over and Henry was laid to rest, the funeral director brought his personal possessions to Esther and, of course, she broke up again upon seeing the few personal things that were in his possession. There was his lodge ring, his billfold with pictures of the children and Esther, and a picture of those two grey mares. It wasn't very clear for it was yellowed some and faded. There were nine credit cards and the usual things like driver's license, car registration, lodge card, union card, insurance cards, and $3.30. In his coat pocket were three payment books, a roll of Tums and his pocket notebook that he doodled in when he was thinking, or planning, or dreaming. There were the usual notes about remembering to have his car serviced, the TV checked, stopping at the store on the way home, and under that was more doodling and the lines of Robert Frost's beautiful poem. But Henry had re-worded it to read:

"The woods are lovely, dark and deep,
But I have *no more* promises to keep,
Nor miles to go before I sleep."

The funeral director also had some insurance papers to sign in order that Esther might collect Henry's life insurance, and that he might get his money. She signed them in triplicate in her fine, but uncertain hand, "Esther A. Morgan," and she noticed that there was no appropriate line for Henry to sign.

Chapter XVIII
THE TRAGIC CONCLUSIONS

The "Great Society" killed Henry as surely as if they had marched him to the wall and ordered ten riflemen to fire a volley into his poor head. His accomplished death was not as sudden or as obvious as all that, but just as sure. The word "society" has been used so often in the preceding pages that perhaps it should be defined. Webster gives it as: "The social order, esp. as a state or system restricting the individual; community life." It is the way of life that was imposed on Henry against his reason and in spite of all his efforts to resist it, by a system bent on the destruction of Henry's freedom and liberty. A system that seeks to enslave cannot tolerate the presence of one free man; so it concludes that all the Henrys must succumb to the system or die.

The tragedy of it all is that Henry died and the real killer was never apprehended or identified in the community in which he lived. He died like a badgered, desperate animal in a cage that society said was of his own choosing. But it was society's way of life that was Henry's killer. They killed him with kindness; liberated him into slavery; prospered him into poverty; freed him into bondage. They reduced him to a tool of his tools; a beast of burden in his own carefully created harness. This is the subtlety — the sheer genius of it all, and such genius can only be the work of some mastermind more cunning than the smartest of men.

The second tragedy is that in spite of the fact that the method of his death has been made known and the identity of his killer exposed, few will ever be made aware of the danger of this destructive system. This tragic drama is being played out in millions of lives around us, and perhaps in our own lives, yet the majority of people in the clutches of the great society will not take the time to read this book, or any other for that matter.

A third tragedy is that of the few who will read it and be alarmed at its message, practically none will do anything about it. Not because they *cannot*, but because they *will not*. Though their heart cries out for liberation, their mind and body are too tired to resist and too accustomed to the "luxuries" of the great society. They are like a great outdoor dog, who, grown accustomed to the security and warmth of the fireside, resents being pushed out into the cold night. He would rather sacrifice his liberty and freedom than give up his indulgence.

A famous classical scholar, in describing the decline and fall of the Grecian and Roman empires, said, "In the end, more than they wanted freedom, they wanted security, a comfortable life, and they lost ALL . . . security, and comfort and freedom." Like them, we are being institutionalized, regimented and enslaved by a "something for nothing" philosophy that is destroying us all by the weapons of our own greed. The great society stands by with its cleverly conceived credit system that allows us to spend our way to slavery while being denied even the pleasure of enjoying that which enslaves us.

Recently it was announced that science was working on a way to preserve men's brains in glass jars after death. These jars are to be filed away and connected to a giant computer which would continue to feed electronic impulses to the brains and keep them "alive." It is said that every "experience" of life can be duplicated and experienced by the brain through electronic impulses. It seems to me that we have just about perfected this system already. Our brains are fed electronic signals through radio and TV; all of our thinking is done for us;

our course of action is decided by the pressure of an electronic age, and the only difference, as I see it, is that they have done us the favor of leaving our brains in our bodies, while constantly controlling them. We are fast becoming a generation of intellectual morons. Like children, we find ourselves repeating the tired jingles and off-color stories of last night's TV, and the empty sayings of the "great" men quoted in last night's paper, whose names we cannot remember. Most of us go through this computerized life without an original thought or a mental or heart conviction about anything. The average man on the street cannot engage in any conversation whose subject ranges beyond the content of yesterday's radio, TV or newspaper. His buying choices are already made subconsciously for him, and he is swept along by this present society in a pre-determined course arbitrarily decided by others. He is afraid to question, challenge, or even suspect the rightness of the world around him and if he does, he is branded as a reactionary— a fanatical trouble maker. He accepts as a way of life that which he hates and abandons without a fight that which he loves. He succumbs to the influence of present day brain washing like a man under drugs. He is institutionalized early in life, and freedom of thought or action is only an empty dream. He is told, "You can't fight progress" until he believes it, and told also that all progress is good for him whether he can appreciate it or not. He lives in a make-believe world that trusts in the ultimate good of society and is kept going by the stupid belief that society is looking out for his interests and will see to it that he "never had it so good."

The freethinkers are fast disappearing from the modern scene for they are the only menace to this system. The daily papers, the TV and radio news reports boast that they are serving the best interest of the "best informed" generation in history. Best informed of what? What good does all this vast daily news work in us except to saturate our already overburdened heart and mind with all the ills of all men everywhere and so further involve us? Few of us have heard anything through the news media of our time that added one inch to our stature or helped us to be better men or women in this life. If we have read the sickening details of one war, rape, robbery, murder, riot or famine or heard the gory details of one senseless automobile crash, what shall it profit us if we hear of a thousand more? Will our being better informed prevent the further happenings of such things? Few of us ever received a letter of which the contents were worth the postage or a telephone call that conveyed a message worthy of the men, machines, money, time, energy and life wasted in the vast complex system of electronic genius needed to convey it to our home.

The greatest waste in life is life itself. It is synonymous with time and is priceless, yet the people of our day spend it as easily for nothing as they do the money they have not yet earned. We are all wrapped up in a feverish endeavor to solve the problems of livelihood, and have only come up with a solution far more complicated than the problem itself. We labor on desperately to liberate ourselves and only succeed in enslaving ourselves by our newfound liberty.

That the technological and material advance in the past 75 years has been astounding, none can deny; but it is time that we sober up from our materialistic binge long enough to tell the next generation what a fantastic price we have paid in mental, physical, and moral involvement. We have paid for it with the real meat of life itself, and are left with the empty shell. Jesus said that a man's life did not consist in the things he possessed, but no one heard Him. We have heard Him, but we do not believe Him; and we have never quite learned that a man is rich in proportion to the number of things he can afford to leave alone in this life.

We are told by the super salesmen of this instant insanity called the "Great Society" that our great advances have lengthened the life span of man by 25 or 30 years. A noteworthy achievement, I am sure, but would it be out of reason to inquire as to what our lives have been saved *for?* We are told by the hawkers of this master delusion that "we never had it so good." Good for what, I might ask of them? They tell us we never had so much leisure time. To be spent on what? We live out of our medicine cabinets on vitamins, tranquilizers and pep pills to get us through the day and then, when we fall into bed exhausted, we lie there wound up like a dollar watch. We dare not sleep too soundly; for at any moment our night may turn to day in a brilliant flood of electric light, or the phone by our bed might call us to further mental and emotional complexities for which we have no capacity, and we may be driven out into the night to our automobile to find ourselves hurtling across the country at 80 miles per hour!

The impressive statistics of the peddlers of this society extol the glories of our high-speed tranportation system; and no one seems to think or care about the fact that upon the bloody altar of this never-satisfied and ugly god we lay thousands of dead bodies annually and hundreds of thousands of broken, twisted, maimed and bleeding ones. All of this, because we have been told that we have the wonderful privilege of getting nowhere fast in order to do nothing when we get there! "Hurry" is the prayer of the devoted, while exhaust fumes contaminate and pollute the air we breathe and eat our lungs away. Billions of dollars annually are sacrificed in the manufacture, repair, maintenance and improvement of this mechanical Frankenstein that is fast devouring our farm lands and vomiting them out in never-ending streams of asphalt and concrete jungles. This is only *one* of this society's "blessings" that threatens to "bless" us into oblivion at 80 miles per hour!

One last sobering thought comes to mind as I conclude this section: being the creatures of habit we are, what inheritance shall we pass on to our children? We are concerned about their education, and the material fortune we can leave them; but what about the legacy of a way of life? We do not seem to remember that as we walk our feet are creating upon the impressionable earth a path that, although we are long gone, our children will continue to follow without a thought or reason in regard to the rightness of it.

The time to do something is *now*. Yesterday has been swallowed by the gulping mouth of time, and tomorrow is only an illusion. We must not continue to live this hectic life without some thought about the awful harvest we are reaping. Let us be sure as we march to its frantic cadence, that we are hearing the right drummer. Let us also recall that Thomas Jefferson said, "The price of liberty is eternal vigilance"; and, if we have any liberty left, let us make it our life's business to be vigilant lest we lose it.

Chapter XIX

LIGHT IN THE DARKNESS

All of us should find ourselves, in some degree or other, in the story of Henry and Esther. Indeed, the purpose of the story was to reveal the influence the great society has achieved in each of us. Portions of it are really the story of my own struggle against this intangible monster system. It is a composite picture of all of us and explains many of the unexplained things in life.

For instance, I have often wondered why certain people are fascinated with antiques as such. Most of them are not usable in any practical degree, nor will they ever be again. They are old, broken, useless and without any real value to anyone. In spite of these facts, thousands of people are not only fascinated, but seemingly obsessed with them. They are sold for fantastic prices and resold at greater prices. They are cherished by those who own them and sought by those who do not. The story of Henry and Esther holds the key to this minor mystery. It is the subconscious longing of man for a more serene and peaceful life than he has known. The obsession with antiques is only one of the many symptoms of this longing. It is the homesickness for a way of life that smolders in each of us; and, by this means, some have found a way to make a physical identification with a way of life they imagine to contain the elements of peace, quiet and rest they desire.

This story explains the camping fever that sweeps the country every spring when people invest thousands of dollars for self-contained camping trailers that they can hook behind their automobile and tow away to some "Whispering Pines" for a week-end to "get away from it all." Others, not able to go in such high fashion, bring along a small tent and oil light, lie beneath the stars and say over and over to no one in particular, "This is really living!" And somehow, it is—for a few days or hours they are at last free of the smothering social claustrophobia that is so real in the routine of their humdrum lives. Here at last, is a chance to be with their families, away from the hypnotism of TV, away from the hum of the wheels of their modern mechanical homes and the monotonous drone of electronic living. Here, for awhile, is a chance to do the things man was made to do: to consider the raven that flies overhead and the lily that grows in the field; to go to the ant and learn her ways and wisdom; and to sit at the feet of God's teachers in nature and learn the real and everlasting lessons of life itself. Here "away from it all" a man can meditate on the heavens above him and reflect on the glory of God and His handiwork (Luke 12:16-34, Proverbs 6:6, Psalms 8:3-9, 19:1-6). "Sad" is only a meager descriptive word to explain the sight of scores of campers, late on Sunday night, wearily making their way back to the drudgery and madness of the great society, while wishing they could camp forever.

The very fact that they *go* back is an important clue in unravelling this complex problem. *Why do* they go back? Among the many reasons is the most satisfactory of all, a spiritual reason. Lot of old, as he fled Sodom, could not stand the thought of being alone in the mountain with God and pled for the relief of a "little city." We seek the escape from the presence of God in the maddening pace of the great society. We may argue against this, but it is solemnly true. A careful study of Genesis 4 will reveal that this is so. Cain, after being rejected of God because of his refusal to do the will of God, fled from the presence of the Lord to a city of his own making in the land of Nod, or *wandering*. There, amidst the bustle and noise of the city, he found a temporary relief from the convicting presence of the Lord. But we will look at his city later on. Suffice to say that the life Henry and Esther first lived is a life that brings man in daily confrontation with God. His handiwork all around us, His glory in every star-spattered sky, His power and voice in the peal of thunder and the flash of jagged lightning, His peace in every riffling brook and shady nook . . . this is the constant revelation of Himself in every part of the earth and heaven that makes natural man uncomfortable and restless; for he knows that all of life is bringing him to a final face-to-face meeting with God. For this cause, the great society finds a fertile field in the deceitful and desperately wicked heart of man. As Adam hid behind the trees in the garden from the voice of God, so modern man hides behind the gadgets, the "things" of this affluent society. Under the background hum of the electronic age, man is seeking refuge from that final confrontation with God. Satan's masterpiece of strategy of the great society of today is his most successful venture since the seed of it was sown in Eve's heart with the lie, "Ye shall not die . . . ye shall be as gods." And so, the promise of every time and labor-saving device, and the power of a universal credit system that places them all within reach of every man, have made us as gods . . . self-sufficient, rich, increased in goods and in need of nothing!

I said the great society was Satan's masterpiece, and it is. Why did he conceive it? What is its motive, and what does it seek to do to all of us? In order to understand this, we must get God's intention for man on this earth clear in our hearts and minds. How did God intend for man to live, and what was he made to do in this life? Let us see in the book of beginnings.

In Genesis it is recorded that in the beginning man was put in a garden God Himself had planted. Out of the ground of that garden God made every tree pleasant to the sight and good for food. He also placed the tree of life and the tree of knowledge of good and evil there. In God's garden east of Eden, or *delight*, there was a river whose purpose was to continually water that garden; and then, dividing into four parts, to flow out of the garden to make fruitful and to bless the entire earth. Man was placed there to live and to work. His labor was to dress the garden and to keep it. Yes, man was intended, in his original state of innocence, *to work!* There is, however, a difference in the work of Paradise and the work of man in a sin-cursed creation. The work of Paradise was a pleasure and a delight that made the garden to yield its most precious fruit: *contentment*. The work of man in the cursed earth is by the sweat of his face and a drudgery that ever reminds him of his need of eternal rest. Paradise gave all that a man needed to live: food, clothing, and shelter. God, in His goodness, gave to Adam His greatest gift: a heaven-made, divinely chosen companion, Eve, whose labor was one of love to be his helpmeet. Her calling in life was to help Adam in his loneliness, that he might be enabled to dress and keep the garden as God intended.

Whatever perspective you may have regarding man in his original state, of this much we are certain: he was intended to live in utter simplicity, depending on God through nature to provide for the necessities of life. The animals were all placed in subjection to Adam for his use and need. The earth was to be subdued by man, and his dominion was to embrace every part of the land, air and sea. The trees and the herb-bearing seed were to feed man and beast, and there in the simplicity of such a life Adam would find time to walk with God in the cool of the day. There was to be an affinity between nature and man; and a semblance of it exists today, for Paul assures us of it in the 8th chapter of Romans. We are told that the whole creation groans and travails in pain together with us, who groan within ourselves, for the release from the bondage of corruption, and groan *for* the glorious liberty of the children of God. It has long been common knowledge that all of the animal kingdom responds to the authority and dominion of man over it. Just recently it has been discovered that plant life also responds to man and manifests such emotions as fear, affection and subjection to him. Nothing was overlooked in God's original plan to make man's life a joy and to give to him, through this way of life, the perfect contentment for which he was created.

God's purpose in this arrangement in regard to Himself is also clearly established in Genesis. We see the hint of it in the name by which He calls Himself often in that book: "The Lord God." The name "God," or "Elohim," means *strong one* and implies also, *faithfulness*. The name "Lord" means the *self-revealing one*. So, in the combined names God is pleased to use to describe Himself in regard to man's way of life, we find the meaning, "the strong and faithful One Who will reveal Himself." This self-revelation of God to man was to be by the manner of life man lived in that garden. In the provision of every good thing in life and by the simplicity of Adam's life in the garden, God would show His faithfulness to His creation, His strength sufficient for our weakness, and hence, reveal His eternal love for man. The blessed result of such a revelation of God would be the fellowship between them that was expressed in God's desire to walk with man in the cool of the day.

Modern day psychologists say that happiness is analyzed as three-part: something to do; something to hope for; and someone to love. God graciously provided for all three in this first arrangement. The days of Adam's life were passed in dressing and keeping the garden, which gave him something to do. They were passed in the hope of the evening that would yield the most precious fruit of all, a walk with God to refresh his tired body. All of his days were passed in the reality of God's eternal and divine love and Eve's undying love and devotion that met his every emotional and physical loneliness.

This way of life was modified, but not revoked, when sin entered the race. To this way of life was added, as a result of sin, a curse upon the serpent; enmity between the serpent and woman; multiplied sorrow in conception; complete subjection of the woman to the man; the earth cursed so that it brought forth thorns and thistles in rebellion to Adam; and sweat added to Adam's face. This change was to follow him through all of life, and he was to return in physical death to the earth from which he was taken. Beyond all of this, Adam was driven from the garden of Paradise he had known to till the ground from whence he was taken; and Paradise lost was guarded by cherubims with a flaming sword lest man eat of the tree of life and live forever in his cursed state. Death must be the logical end of Adam in his sinful state so that a new beginning might be made. That beginning was made in the life of the Lord Jesus Christ which was freely given to man on the cross of Calvary.

Chapter XX

ORIGIN OF THE GREAT SOCIETY

What caused Adam to lose the Paradise God made for him? What cost Adam his contented way of life, marked by peace, plenty and the precious presence and personal fellowship of God? What kind of life replaced this perfect way of life? This is where Satan, the arch-enemy of God, entered the scene. I said, in the story of Henry and Esther, that such a clever, subtle and powerful system must have the genius of some mastermind behind it. That genius and mastermind is Satan. From the moment of man's happy entry to Paradise, Satan sought the destruction of that man and his way of life. Man was enjoying what Satan had been deprived of; and so the eternal envy and jealousy of that old serpent plotted his destruction, and he has labored through every generation to destroy all men and their way of life. We hear the philosophy of his great society in his hissing words, "Ye shall not die . . . ye shall be as gods." He promised abundance of pleasure, food, knowledge and wisdom; and when Eve picked that forbidden fruit, the "something for nothing" way of life was born. Immediately following this sin, they were cunningly diverted from their true labor in life to sewing fig leaves in an effort to ease their circumstances, to beautify themselves and to hide them from the presence of God. Their sin produced a state, or way of life, that in order to maintain, would enslave them to works never intended for them. The result of this satanic way of life was to so occupy their minds, bodies and souls, that they would have no more time or inclination to hear God's word, or walk with Him in the cool of the day. The final fruit of it all was to change their hearts toward God from love to fear, from openness and freedom to hiding behind the trees, and from a desire to walk with Him to a losing of themselves in the complexities of life.

Cain's solution to the whole matter speaks for all of Adam's seed. Only redeemed man can continue long in the simplicity of life with contentment. Abel found redemption in the blood of the lamb, and hence contentment and freedom from the involvements of Satan's way of life; but Cain, because of his rejection of Calvary prophesied, was rejected by God. Destined to be a vagabond and a fugitive for the rest of life, he sought refuge in the carefully planned place provided for man by Satan: the city. Once the earth had yielded its strength to Cain when he tilled the soil; but now it withheld its fruit by divine intervention so that Cain might be brought to repentance. If he had continued in God's way of life, he would have been driven to the atoning sacrifice; for life would have no meaning apart from the presence and knowledge of God.

Cain fled to the land of Nod, or *wandering*, and built a city. It is significant that Cain passed on a way of life to his children that would destine them to the same estrangement that he knew.*

***Author's note:**
You are no doubt reminded that God did bless and use a city in the case of Jerusalem, city of peace, and promises that our eternity with Jesus will be passed in a city, the New Jerusalem. How does this fit in with the origin of the city? Are all cities Satanic and evil? The Jerusalem of Biblical times was the only city where God ever placed His name. It was the only city that was blessed with the presence of God Himself in the form of the Shekinah glory that filled the holy of holies in the great temple built for God. It was a city whose rule was theocratic, and every facet of the life in that city was designed to bring man face to face with God in the sacrificial altar of His temple. The new Jerusalem will be the eternal home of the saints, and I only remark in passing that the characteristics which singled out the original Jerusalem from all the cities of earth will prevail again. Look at John's description of that blessed place and see that it is not a city at all, in the sense of cities as we know them; but it is the Paradise once lost by Adam regained at last. Our eternal enjoyment of its way of life is secured forever by the blood of Jesus Christ, God's sacrificial Lamb. Look closely and see that all the original effects of sin are gone: no more tears, death, sorrow, crying, or pain. The pure river of the water of life flows gently in its midst; the tree of life bursting with 12 manner of fruit and healing leaves; and the curse lifted forever. No night, no artificial lighting, not even the light of nature will be required. The light, the glory, the beauty and perfection of that place will be the Lord Jesus Christ Himself.

Genesis 4 tells the story. This city was a place of music, harp and organ, of brass and iron. This thriving society was not dependent on God for anything, but upon their corporate ability to manufacture all they needed, and to entertain their impoverished souls with the fine arts. Hence, it was a godless society composed of men united in their common desire to escape the presence of the Lord. Together they could depend on each other for strength, protection, comfort and happiness. They would never need to till the soil and be cast upon the mercy of God to open His Heaven for rain, or to shine His sun upon their lifeless seed. The abundance of their materialistic society was god enough for them; and so the living, faithful God Who wanted only to reveal Himself to man in love, peace, and joy was replaced by the god of this world: Satan. The ruin of their way of life is evident to every reader of scripture. Their "perfect" city was so filled with violence, sexual abuse, and disorder, that in a few short years, we read that God's commentary on this "progress" was that the wickedness of man was great; and that in every imagination of his, the thoughts of his heart were only evil continually. The sad and inevitable end was that it repented God that He had ever made man, for man grieved Him at His heart. The grieved and lonely God looked at the madness of the great society, heard its throbbing jungle beat, saw its smokestacks, its insanity and knew that His certain destruction must come. And it did. (Read all of Genesis 4-6.)

This great society, first instituted by men seeking relief from the presence of the Lord and masterminded by Satan to so occupy their bodies, souls and minds that they could not have time or inclination to seek and know God, has enlarged itself through the years. The masterpiece of deception, the crowning glory of all of Satan's genius is in the full-grown monster of the materialism of our time.

And rightly so, for the society of our time is unique in that it is the forerunner of the perfected kingdom of Satan to be ruled over by the Beast, the man of sin and son of perdition that will come.

The prophetic scriptures foresee a last, great, anti-God system that will eventually rule the entire earth. The last great ruler, The Beast, will be a ruthless despot who causes the vast power of his kingdom to crush any resistance to it. This future rule will be so terrible, and the resultant judgment upon it so severe, that unless the time of its existence had been shortened by God there would be no flesh left. The tempo of our times beats out the message that we are being hurtled into the reality of that kingdom of darkness as fast as our super-speed civilization can carry us. We look around us and see that we are passengers on a collision course, locked on our suicidal mission by the prince of the power of the air. The increasing involvement of body, mind and soul is the evidence that Satan is pressing for one last victory before Jesus Christ returns to destroy that old serpent whose head was crushed at Calvary. The victory he wants is to hurtle this generation to hell under the hypnotism of TV; the plenty of their materialism; the mind control of his super-salesmen; the body control of a vast drug addiction in the form of pain, stress, tension, insomnia, and nervousness relief-offering drugs; and the supposed security of a false religious system that lulls us to sleep with its pipe organ and soft pews.

We need a prophet with the rough garments of camelskin and a diet, not of Coke and hot dogs, but of locusts and wild honey; one who has been alone with God in the wilderness and who has seen this age through the eyes of God. We need an Elijah, or a John the Baptist, who will insult us, alarm us, awaken us and stir us to free ourselves from the entanglements of this life and look with renewed hope to the soon coming of our Lord Jesus Christ. But, a prophet must have the authority of God's word to persuade the people of the authenticity of his message. Surely, if this present way of life is a masterpiece of satanic delusion, and if it is unique to our times (and all must admit that until 50-60 years ago, life was practically unchanged since Bible times), then surely the prophetic scriptures foresaw this great society that destroyed Henry and Esther and threatens all of us.

Chapter XXI

HISTORY OF THE GREAT SOCIETY

The phenomenon of all that I write about is clearly predicted in the Holy Scriptures. If you have eyes to read it, ears to hear it and above all, a heart that is willing to see it and be disturbed because of our involvement in this satanic system, it will be quite apparent in God's word. The prophetic word tells of an unannounced time that will see the departure of God's people from this earth in a mass exodus that we often refer to as the "Rapture" (I Thess. 4:13-18). This catching away of the saints by the Lord Jesus Christ will be accomplished as He "descend(s) from Heaven with a shout, with the voice of the archangel, and with the trump of God." After this departure, the Beast will be unhindered in his desire to control the world. The Rapture of the New Testament saints at that time is a striking similarity to the great exodus of Israel from the bondage of Egypt. If there is any prophetic significance in that event that would help us to see what the Rapture would mean for us, then there must be some prophetic light in the events in Israel's lives *prior* to the Rapture, or exodus. Paul assures us that these things happened to them for our admonition.

Just before the mass exodus of Israel in the night by the power of God, there was a satanic strategy unfolded against the saints. You may read this for yourself in Exodus, chapter one. The satanic strategy was one that deepened their bondage in their way of life. Taskmasters were appointed to afflict them with burdens; they were forced to build *cities* that housed the materialistic treasures of the present world system; they were made to serve with rigour, or do the work of slaves; their lives were made bitter with hard bondage in the materialism of mortar and brick; and population control by the state was instituted. All of these familiar signs mark our times today, none dare deny.

The people of God were groaning because of their bondage, chapter 2 tells us; and God heard them, remembered, looked upon them and had respect unto them. Moses came and challenged the system with "Let my people go," to which the great society answered with more work, more burdens, and economic pressures. Bear in mind this was all worked so that God's people would have no time for the worship of God. When Moses insisted upon freedom for the people, the system offered a series of compromises. These same compromises appear when we, today, become alarmed with the similarity of the Israelites' lives prior to the exodus and our lives now. First, the compromise that said, "Stay in the system and live for God." Next, if that offer fails to entice us or satisfy our restlessness to break the shackles of involvement, "Go out of the system a little way, but not too far. Don't escape the power of the system." The third compromise followed, "Go out, but leave your little ones here. Live like you want to, but don't impose your way of life on your children." The last offer of the satanic system was, "Go out, but give up all your materialistic possessions—leave your goods behind." The Israelites were victorious only when they were allowed to go, take their little ones and all their possessions with them to the glory of God. There is too clear a likeness to our own times in this portion of the scriptures to deny the prophetic warning.

Then, if you will, look at Daniel's prophecy that foresaw the end times and this materialistic, anti-Christian masterpiece of delusion that tells and retells the lie that in our time and labor-saving things we can find all that is only and ultimately found in the Lord Himself. Daniel saw the Beast to come, making war against the saints and prevailing against them; he also saw him "wearing out the saints." The mark of his system is "change" or "progress," and he even changes the times and laws that have stood for centuries. He is prophesied as having the ability to "destroy wonderfully" and his policy causes the crafts to prosper. He shall destroy many by peace, Daniel warns, and his mouth speaks great things. A summary of Daniel's preview of the last world system before Jesus comes shows that it is a complete totalitarian rule where materialism reigns as god. My heart agrees with the above description when I remember Henry and Esther and how the war against Henry by the society around him wore him out; the constant change destroyed him wonderfully; the crafts prospered through his destruction; and the constant sound of the great mouth of that system through his radio, TV and newspaper drowned out the sound of everything around him.

The prophetic word is filled with descriptive phrases that so perfectly describe our way of life that they might have been written by an observer of the 20th century, and indeed they were. From His place in the circle of the universe, beyond the realm of time, God caused holy men of old to speak as they were moved by His Spirit. God observed our times and caused John on the Isle of Patmos to write of our present society in terms that describe the wealth of the merchants because of it and how the system glorified itself and caused men to live deliciously. In Revelation 18 John listed her merchandise as gold, silver, precious stones, pearls, fine linen, purple, silk, scarlet, thyine wood, ivory, precious wood, brass, iron, marble, cinnamon, odours, ointments, frankincense, wine, oil, fine flour, wheat, beasts, sheep, horses, chariots; and last, but not the least of that which the great society of Satan has made merchandise: *the bodies and souls of men.* Who can deny that this is an accurate record of our affluent society?

Read II Peter, the entire second chapter, and hear the charges made against the super-salesmen of Satan's society today by the Holy Spirit. Hear how they promise liberty to the people but only bring them to bondage; how they promise with great swelling words of vanity, like the TV commercials of our time, liberty to all while they themselves are the servants of corruption. Hear how they bring men into entanglement with the pollutions of this world and overcome men, and all of it to turn men from the Lord Jesus Christ.

Hear Paul warning Timothy regarding the last days, not to be entangled with the affairs of this life (II Timothy 2:4). Hear Paul warn him about the snare of Satan in which men are taken captive. Then in II Timothy 3:1-7 read about our times as clearly as though you were reading a newspaper description of our society. Read thoughtfully the second chapter of II Thessalonians and see that our day, as the age of grace ends, will be the age of the "big lie." Reflect, if you dare, upon the frightful fact that all of our present economic system is based on the lie. Most all business is conducted in the power of it. The advertising that sells our merchandise; the salesman that tells about it; the contract with its fine print; the failure of the product to match all its claims; the inability to get the service we were told was "guaranteed;" all of it smacks of the big lie. It forces even those who desire to be honest to become liars in order to survive in this lying age. The philosophy of the whole present society is a lie; the lie that we can "buy now and pay later" and still be free. One day the earth will learn that the present economy is bringing us swiftly to the day prophesied by the word of God as a great time of tribulation that will come upon the whole earth to try it. The *end* of the suicide course we are on at present is the "mark of the beast," without which no man can *buy* or *sell.* I am convinced, dear reader, that that mark, which is the number of his name, could well be a single, universal *credit card.** Without the power of the credit system, Henry would still be living as he should at Whispering Pines. Without its corruption, Henry would have been forced to live within his means, accepting God's supply as the divine estimate of his needs. Without the "buy now, pay later" philosophy, Henry would never have been brought to the bondage that destroyed him.

The tragedy is that many of God's people are being destroyed in their testimony and usefulness, as well as in their fellowship with the Father, by the same means. It took me 20 years to understand that credit buying is seldom God's means of meeting my needs. In most of that type of buying I have done no more than any unsaved man could do, and hence brought no glory to God, but further bondage to myself. I cannot give you any pat answers to this terribly complex problem of how the believer ought to live and conduct himself in this decadent world system. I cannot tell *you* how to live beyond its power. Each of us must be fully persuaded in our *own* heart how our liberty must be sought, but seek it we *must* at any cost. I am determined to be as free as possible of this monster of society around me and seek to glorify God in my way of life as well as in my body and my ministry.

***Author's note:**
The striking description of the "mark" in Revelation 13:7-18 lends credence to such an interpretation. It is said that the Beast will have power over all kindreds, and tongues, and nations (verse 7). All—small and great, rich and poor, free and bond—will be forced to possess this mark. It will be applied to hand or forehead, indicating both classes of society; intellectual and laboring. No man can buy or sell without it; hence, capital and labor are both under the control of it. It is said to be the number of a man, or the sum total of all he is—body, soul and spirit. This is the total control the credit system will eventually exercise over men. One look at the manner in which all of life is being geared to the Social Security number of each man, will suggest that the universal credit card could carry that number. Currency will be a thing of the past; and without it, the last vestige of economic freedom will be forever gone. Man will be forced to buy and sell what he is told, when he is told, where he is told by the Beast; hence, totally controlled by him. God give us wisdom to see the shadow of this system falling over us now, in these last days.

Let us pursue now some guide lines in His word for the seeking of that freedom. That we should even *want* out is a miracle of grace. The enablement to seek some better way of life than we have known; to live in a manner that frees us from the power and influence of such a satanic system, requires a conviction born in the word of God and empowered by the Holy Spirit of God. Generally, there will be two reactions by Christians to this message: (1) Those who will propose that we flee to the wilderness, move away from society and live to ourselves, like hermits or monks, and so escape the corrupting influence of the system that seeks to destroy our way of life. (2) Those who will run to the other pole of extremity and suggest that we are in this world until Jesus comes and that we should just settle down and make the best of it. *Somewhere* between these two extremes there must be a better way. There is a blessed balance of truth in everything that is so much like compromise that the two are often mistaken. Compromise is surrender on the installment plan. The balance I speak of is what Paul pressed on the Ephesians in the sixth chapter. In the 10th verse he exhorts them to be "strong in the Lord, and in the power of His might"; in verse 11 to "Put on the whole armour of God, that ye may be able to *stand* against the wiles of the devil." Verse 12 tells of our enemy—not flesh and blood, but principalities and powers . . . rulers of darkness of this age . . . spiritual wickedness in high places. Then he tells us once more that our only way out is to take the full armour of God and *stand* in the evil day, "and having done all, *stand.*" Verse 14 begins with that word again, "*Stand,* therefore . . . ." The Christian wages no offensive against this satanic system, nor does he fall back in retreat. He *stands!* Though ten thousand may fall at his right hand . . . he stands! Though the principalities and powers come against him with all their spiritual wickedness . . . he stands! God *enables* him to stand . . . steadfast, unmoveable . . . and as a witness against the society in which he finds himself.

When Israel was in Egyptian bondage (a type of our present place in the world system today) a thick darkness had come in all the land, but all the children of Israel had light in their dwellings. When God visited the land in awful judgment and a great cry went up throughout the whole land, not a dog moved his tongue against the people of God, neither man nor beast, for God wanted Israel to know that He had put a difference between the Israelites and the Egyptians (Exodus 10:22-23, 11:6-7).

Jesus prayed in His high priestly prayer, in John 17, for us. In the 15th verse He prayed, "I pray not that thou shouldest take them out of the world (system), but that thou shouldest keep them from the evil. They are not of the world, even as I am not of the world. Sanctify them through thy truth: thy word is truth." Here is the happy balance I speak of. Let us continue *in* this society, but let our lives show once and for all that we are not *of* it. Let us show that we have been delivered from the power, the enchantment, the hypnotism of it. Let there be blessed light in our dwelling that demonstrates that the prince of this world has come, but has nothing in us. Let our lives cry out that our trust is in the living God, not in uncertain materialism; and that He, our blessed and living God, has given us richly all things to enjoy.

Peter assures us that we are a chosen generation, a royal priesthood, an holy nation, a peculiar people, and that our calling in this society is to show forth the praises of Him who hath called us into His marvelous light. This is not done by mere preaching, for we may never get the attention of those about us by this means. There must be something about the way we live and conduct ourselves in this godless society that stamps us as a peculiar people in that we are generally freed from the bondage of this evil system. Peter further tells us that our place in this world is one of "strangers" or "temporary residents" and of "pilgrims" or "traveling foreigners." If this be so, then the way we live and conduct ourselves must be consistent with that position. A temporary resident, a traveling foreigner, would be freed from the involvement of the society around him and walk in such liberty that he would be in a blessed position of testimony concerning the place of his citizenship. Our citizenship is in heaven; and heavenly-mindedness must mark our lives with distinctiveness that testifies *against* the system around us, and witnesses *to* the blessed kingdom of which we are a part. Let us turn from the idols of the corrupt society designed to ruin and bring into bondage God's people, and let us serve the true and living God while we wait for His Son from heaven.

Henry and Esther didn't know the way out, for the way is a PERSON: the Lord Jesus Christ. We know that way if we have rested in His atoning work at Calvary for our sins and God's satisfaction. That way is to walk as He walked in the society around Him with the conscious realization that earth can hold no power over us not given to it from heaven. Jesus has made us free. He has delivered us from the world system and its corrupting influence. Let us walk in the light of that freedom. Let us heed the word of God which cries: "Come out of her, my people, that ye be not partakers of her sins, and that ye receive not of her plagues" (Revelation 18:4). I long, in my own life, to escape the sins of this society; the plagues of her damnable system that afflicts all she touches with the disease of involvement. I long to be more than a slave chained to the galley of constant involvement in this life. I long to be free in my time, body, mind, possessions and family life that I might truly serve the Lord Jesus and love Him as I ought. May the Lord Jesus show each of us how this can be obtained in our lives to His praise and glory.

Chapter XXII

THE TREASURE HID IN THE FIELD

In I Timothy 6:6-21 we find what I believe to be the most important practical passage in the New Testament on the subject of how a believer should look upon life in this present world. The Rapture, or the appearing of the Lord Jesus in the air to take us *out* of this world, is our daily hope; but we must also occupy until He comes. He left us here to make a testimony to the grace of God in our lives, and we must realize that, until He comes, there is opportunity and time that we must redeem to the glory of God Let us look at Henry and Esther one last time in the light of this blessed passage. You will notice that it is an accurate summary of what happened to them. At the first, they were seeking but food and raiment and had found perfect contentment. At the last, the pressure of the great society upon them, which could not stand the testimony of their contentment against it, caused them to "will to be rich." This brought the promised results: they fell into temptation, a snare, into foolish and hurtful lusts (for more and more things) and at last, Henry drowned in destruction and perdition. This is the devastating effect of the great society upon the unsaved. The results upon the saved are seen in verse 10: erring from the faith and piercing themselves through with many sorrows.

It is possible for a saved person to know the *joy* of the Lord in the forgiveness of his sins, and *peace* with God because of this joy, without ever knowing the *contentment* of the Christian life. It is the difference between joy and happiness. We may know the joy that is unspcakable and full of glory without walking in the happiness of a life freed from the pressure of the world system around us. If you do not know this contentment in life, it is because you are under the delusion that *gain* and *godliness* are synonymous and that contentment is found in materialism. This is the big lie of the great society. When we are conscious that we are not content, not happy, we are told by the world that to possess more and more will change all of this. We are told that the happiness we seek lies beyond the necessities of life. Verse 5 tells us in no uncertain terms that we are to withdraw from those who reason thus. It is godliness *with* contentment that is great gain.

All of us are going to leave this world one day. When we do, we are only going to take *out* with us what we brought *in* with us. NOTHING is the sum total of it. Therefore, the world can add nothing to our contentment. Man is so created as to carry about within himself the blessed ability and potential for happiness that is not dependent upon anything this world has to offer. Man is self-sufficient in the matter of contentment. No material possession can help him attain the happiness his soul longs for. It is found only in godliness, which is salvation and peace in Jesus Christ. If this be true, then it follows that a saved man, who has found this peace with God through Jesus Christ, can find perfect contentment in the necessities of life: food and raiment. (The word "raiment" conveys also the thought of shelter.)

Verse 8 is a wonderful promise! I thought for years it was a command to be content with these meager things, whether we were or not. It is a blessed promise! Perfect contentment, freedom from the enslaving power of this system, is found in the pursuit of only food, clothing, and shelter. The pursuit of anything beyond this will only bring sorrow and will destroy our contentment in life. Contentment can be defined as an "inward self-sufficiency (not sufficient in our*self,* but self-*contained* sufficiency) as opposed to the lack or desire of outward things; to be possessed of an unfailing strength; to suffice; to be able to ward off any danger." It is not joy and peace, but a blessed stream that should flow *from* that joy and peace we have in Christ. It can only flow as we seek the source of that contentment: the necessities of life.

The alternate course for the believer is to will to be rich. When we speak of "rich" we associate it in our minds with great wealth; to be a millionaire; but this is not so in the original. The word simply means "to possess more than is necessary to contentment," that is, more than food, clothing and shelter. The word "will" means "a considered will, not born of emotion, but of reason." This is the source of all of our problems. We find ourselves enmeshed in the gears of a godless system; some of us in debt beyond any hope of recovery; brought to slavery of mind, body and soul because of it; simply because we reasoned that contentment could be found in that which lay beyond the necessities of life. We deliberately desired, willed, lusted, or pursued that which was beyond the realm of contentment, and we have reaped the certain sorrow God promises for it. Think back how many times you sat down and set your mind to a determined plan to possess that which you knew you could live without, but felt it would add to the contentment of life. You knew it was beyond your means; yet you pursued it anyway and came back with it to learn you had been deceived once more. You paid the price a thousand times in contentment destroyed and happiness spoiled. This passage is true and is the secret to our distress.

Listen to a composite picture of those under such delusion: they fall helplessly without warning into temptation or danger; they are taken in a snare like fish are taken in a net; they fall helplessly into foolish lusts or into silly, stupid, senseless desires that do nothing but hurt them; they drown, sink, plunge, or, as the Greek will properly convey, are "swamped" in ruin and waste. The desire to have more than that which is necessary to the pursuit of the necessities of life is to seek a self-sufficiency based on materialism, not an inward godliness; and it is the root of all evil. It can cause Christians to err from the faith, or to be led astray and seduced and made to wander about spiritually; and will, if pursued, pierce them with many sorrows; that is, will wound them with thorny grief, untold agony and acute mental pangs.

What shall we do to prevent this from happening further in our lives? Verses 11 and 12 give the three F's of freedom. *Flee,* like a man from a burning house or an attacking lion, from further involvement and the desire to possess more than you need for life. *Follow,* or pursue righteousness, godliness, faith, love, patience, meekness; that is: walk in the spirit. *Fight* the good fight of faith. Lay hold on eternal life. Now, if you are saved, you already have eternal life through Jesus Christ our Lord, but Paul is pressing upon us the idea that we should lay hold of the life we possess. Get hold of the meaning of it . . . realize the power of it . . . walk in the liberty of it. The original would stand this meaning: lay hold on the real meaning of life, or on what living really is. Really living is godliness with contentment; freedom from the madness of materialism; liberty from the enslavement of mind, body and soul to enjoy what living is all about! Jesus came to give us life and that we might have it more abundantly.

And so, my story is about ended. If I hid a treasure and then told you where to find it, only faith would be required to search for it there. God has hidden the contentment and happiness of life in the lawful pursuit of food, clothing and shelter and that which pertains to that realm. If we long for it enough, we will search for it there and we will surely find it—as surely as God's promises are true: "Seek and ye shall find," "Knock and it shall be opened unto you," "Learn of me and ye shall find rest for your souls." These are all the words of our blessed Lord Jesus assuring us that it is so. What a testimony it would be to see believers living in the midst of a godless society, yet unentangled in its net; to see them quietly pursuing the necessities of life, but aloof from the madness of desire that characterizes our time; to see them at peace with God and each other and unspotted by the world around them; to see them content with just the necessities of life and possessed of an ability to find peace and happiness in the simple things of life. Henry and Esther, though unsaved, knew this secret once; and it explains why even the unsaved who live a simple life are oftentimes more content than the believer trying to keep up with the progress of a satanic society. Oh, to see this in the lives of God's people is my prayer and heart's desire!—to see them amidst the pressure and flow of the course of the world, STANDING, unmoved, unbowed, unbent . . . not conformed, but *transformed* by the renewing of their minds in Jesus Christ . . . loving mankind around them, and living in the genuine demonstration of that love . . . following a manner of life because it yields the precious fruit of contentment and joy, not because "everybody else" lives that way . . . adapting their lives, not to the pressures of society, but to the pressures of the Holy Spirit within. This is the kind of preaching that will open hearts to hear from our mouths the word of God. If our lives are like the bush aflame, men will turn out of the way to inquire as to our secret. What course will you now take in the light of this truth? Will the message of this book be like the voice of John the Baptist—a cry in the wilderness of our lives—bringing us to repentance and faith, in a whole new way of life? Or will it be like the plaintive note of Henry's whippoorwill . . . lost in the hum of society's wheels? Only each of us in the secret place of our heart can decide. Only the Holy Spirit can enable us to do what we have decided.

★ ★ ★

"But godliness with contentment is great gain. For we brought nothing into this world, and it is certain we can carry nothing out. And having food and raiment let us be therewith content. But they that will be rich fall into temptation and a snare, and into many foolish and hurtful lusts, which drown men in destruction and perdition. For the love of money is the root of all evil: which while some coveted after, they have erred from the faith, and pierced themselves through with many sorrows.

"But thou, O man of God, flee these things; and follow after righteousness, godliness, faith, love, patience, meekness. Fight the good fight of faith, lay hold on eternal life, whereunto thou art also called, and hast professed a good profession before many witnesses. I give thee charge in the sight of God, who quickeneth all things, and before Christ Jesus, who before Pontius Pilate witnessed a good confession; that thou keep this commandment without spot, unrebukeable, until the appearing of our Lord Jesus Christ: which in His times He shall shew, who is the blessed and only Potentate, the King of kings and Lord of lords; Who only hath immortality, dwelling in the light which no man can approach unto; Whom no man hath seen, nor can see: to Whom be honour and power everlasting. Amen.

"Charge them that are rich in this world, that they be not highminded, nor trust in uncertain riches, but in the living God, who giveth us richly all things to enjoy; that they

do good, that they be rich in good works, ready to distribute, willing to communicate; laying up in store for themselves a good foundation against the time to come, that they may lay hold on eternal life.

"O Timothy, keep that which is committed to thy trust, avoiding profane and vain babblings, and oppositions of science falsely so called: which some professing have erred concerning the faith. Grace be with thee. Amen."

(I Timothy 6:6-21)

THE END